Tony C

BAULOX

BRANDON

First published 1983
Brandon Book Publishers Ltd
Dingle, Co. Kerry, Ireland

British Library Cataloguing in Publication Data

Cafferky, Tony
  Baulox.
  I. Title
  823' .914(F)   PR6053.A/

  ISBN 0—86322—021—5
  ISBN 0—86322—020—7 Pbk

This book is published with the financial assistance
of the Arts Council/An Chomhairle Ealaíon, Ireland.

Map: Brian Kelly

Typesetting: Printset & Design Ltd

Printed by Biddles Ltd, Guildford, England

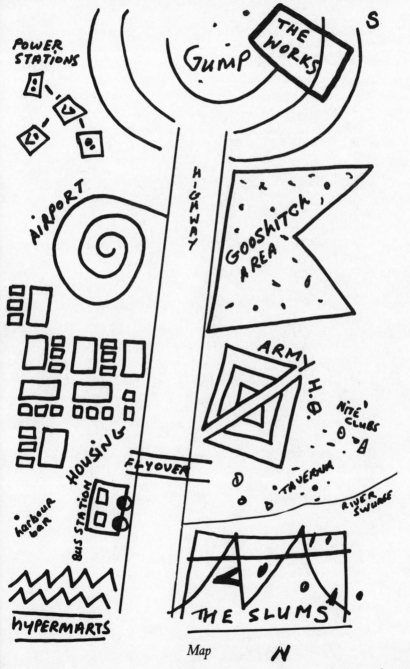

Map

Part One

Daf Ghoosterdoost!
(The Beginning)

One

He batters in the skull of the boiled egg with the bubbly end of the
spoon, turns to me, mischief twinkling in his watery blue eyes, and says,
"Paddy, did you ever contemplate going to Baulox?"

"What!" says I. I'm sitting about ten inches away from him, trying
to concentrate on the dog results in the morning paper. It's a highly
awkward and contrarious thing having the breakfast with the da – I
can't even wake myself up before he starts coming out with the wildest
of notions. Sure, only a few mornings ago wasn't he telling me he had a
job lined up for me as a Junior Assistant in the Archives. Holy Snot! My
heart nearly went disordered when I heard that, together with a lot of
stuff about A Secure Pension Scheme For Groupies, and A Safe Hedge
Against The Galloping Inflation. There I was, barely seventeen, and he
was outrageously suggesting I should doddle away the rest of my days in
the Registry of Mortgages. Obviously he wanted me to quit living
altogether and go to work.

"Baulox?" asks I incredulously. Of course the baldy headed eejit
says nothing for a moment, drawing at my curiosity and letting his eyes
go off on the twinkle again. He loves to do that – startle me with some
preposterous suggestion during the opening hours of the day and then
letting me stew for ages before arriving at an explanation.

"Baulox!" says I again.

"Oh balderdash!" he says, getting horribly huffy with his boiled
egg. As usual most of the yellow stuff had dribbled down the side of the
shell onto the table. After the ma died he couldn't do anything right
except polish his shoes.

"Why don't you cook the bloody yoke before you eat it?" says I. He
ignores this advice as if I had said nothing at all.

"One of my best clients lives in Baulox," he says, scrawbing about
in the eggshell looking for more yellow.

"And so bleeding what?" says I.

Two

NATURALLY I DON'T GIVE A FIDDLER'S ELBOW WHERE THE DA'S CLIENTS LIVE
BUT LATER THAT DAY WHEN I'M OFF DRINKING WITH JODY AND THE LADS
THEY TELL ME I'M OUT OF MY BOX MISSING A GLORIOUS OPPORTUNITY LIKE
THIS.

Naturally I couldn't give a fish's tit where his clients live. These are the
pale men in the dark suits that go scuttering around the Registry of
Mortgages looking for information to put in their briefcases. And this
particular client that lives in Baulox is what the da calls a very important
man – he is a millionaire more than four or five times and owns a
colossal big factory. He calls himself Herr Blumm, and for reasons of his
own he told the da he would fix me up with a job in return for a small
favour. What the favour is the da won't tell me because I give all my
inside information to Micko who is a part-time revolutionary.

He can stick his job up his arse is my formal attitude but later that day
when I'm out drinking with the lads they tell me I'm off my rocker.
Seemingly this was an opportunity that I had been waiting for all my life,
and Jody himself would have gone to Baulox like the proverbial bleeding
light.

"D'ye know what, Paddy?" he says. (We're on our fourth pint in
The Long Bar at the time.) I sort of look at him quizzically as the da puts
it.

"What?" says I.

"I'd love to go to Baulox," he says. And that made me think because
if Jody wanted to go, so did I. And before I knew what was going on I
was ringing up the da in the Registry to tell him to get me a ticket and
the lads were arranging a going away party. Jody doesn't like the long
finger so of course we have to have the party that very afternoon. We all
pile out of the pub in very high spirits – Micko, Hairlips, Stabber, Jody,
myself and the rest of the lads, but we're no sooner on the pavement
when we find ourselves on what the ma used to call the horns of
dilemma. Jody wants the party to be held out at the Bull Wall – out on
the beach where we can go for midnight swims and shout our heads off
without the uncalled for interference of catholics and cops. But Micko
opts for Howth Head where the magic mushrooms are and where we can
make a raid on some English Lord's Castle and build a monster bonfire.

Naturally then we all have to wait to get the final word from Hairlips. Lips never spews out more than a few words at a time and this gives him maximum room for wiser decisions.

"What do you think, Hairlips?" asks Stabber.

"Yea?" says Pidgeon, but Hairlips doesn't say anything for a while. He's thinking. We're stopped on one of the side streets at the back of Matt Talbot's church, and I can see Jody is looking around to see if there is a car we can borrow for the occasion. Finally Hairlips gives us the gen – "It's a question of appropriation, and considering all things, the sea would be more than appropriate."

And that settles that though I think we're all wondering why the sea is more appropriate than a mountain for a going away party. But we don't ask any useless questions. Jody liberates a small Japanese car and we drive off in the general direction.

"I don't know what we'd do without you, Jody," says Pidgeon, admiring his driving abilities as we skid around onto the North Strand highway.

"No bother," says Jody who's been liberating cars since he was eleven with a little gadget he made out of a metal coat hanger.

"Another victory for public transport," says Micko who the da tells me is an irresponsible communist which makes me all the more proud to know him. He's an apprentice electrician that can do anything with electrics – he was born in a fuse box because it was his great grandfather from Ballina that invented electricity before they sent it to school. I remember when we were kids together he used to play tricks on the local police by rewiring their computers and walkie talkies and getting them very irritable and confused running around after all the wrong leads. Not that we do that sort of thing any more for we're nearly grown up now, and Micko is doing a steady line with a girl from Crumlin.

"What about the girls?" says Micko.

"Let's leave them out of this," says Jody overtaking a blue Mercedes and giving the driver a blast of the horn and the victory signal. Jody has six or seven sisters and that makes him a bit of a sexist at times. On we go out by Fairview and of course Pidgeon and Stabber get around to asking what sort of alcohol we're going to be drinking. Pidgeon and Stabber are our alcoholics and they come from very long lines – anyone who was ever in either of their families was a hopeless alcoholic and most of their relations are up in the looney bin drying themselves out for the big binge when they're freed. We do an investigation into our pockets to determine our financial standing but it's not up to much, so Jody suggests we liberate some beer from one of the rugby and cricket clubs. We all agree that that's the only feasible solution, and ten minutes later he drives us up the lane to The Hookers R&C Club (Dancing on Saturday Nights – Members Only). There's nobody around except the gardener because Micko tells us all the members are off working in the banks.

Stabber and Pidgeon go off to spoof up the gardener and ask him about grass seeds and distract him while the rest of us go off hunting for some beer. It only takes us a minute to locate dozens of barrels in the dressing room beside the bar. We borrow two of them although Micko thinks we should take five. "It wouldn't be fair," says Micko, "if all those bankers had to drink so much beer and then run around after that eggball they use."

We settle for three barrels then for Jody doesn't want to bend the springs on his new car.

"You're only borrowing it for the day," says Micko.

"Agh! Those Japanese cars aren't up to much," says Jody.

"What do you think, Hairlips?" asks Micko, but Lips doesn't think it's important enough to give it consideration. So we just load the barrels into the boot, wave goodbye to the gardener and roll on out to the sea. It's what Jody calls an orderly start to a wild party but I don't remember too much about it.

Three

IT'S THE BEST PARTY JODY EVER WENT TO BUT I DON'T REMEMBER A THING ABOUT IT EXCEPT WAKING UP THE FOLLOWING AFTERNOON IN AN ENGLISHMAN'S TENT OUTSIDE GALWAY.

The da is always telling me that drink is an overestimated pastime, and he's right when you have a black hole in your head the morning after with no memories of the good times in it. I haven't a clue how we got to Galway. We hitched back after returning the car to outside a Japanese factory. We all agreed it was an excellent party and I kept an ear open to try and fill in the blanks. There was mention of us borrowing a boat, and Pidgeon falling overboard, and being saved by Micko, and an all night drive across Ireland, and some Englishman who decided he was going to spend the night in an hotel. And that's all. Naturally I wasn't going to tell the lads my head wasn't working properly.

There was a lot of handshakes then, and next thing is don't I find myself traipsing down to the Airport Bus with the da's honeymoon suitcase and a one-way ticket to Baulox.

I was never on an aeroplane before and after my first attempt I wouldn't recommend them at all. Cellophane sandwiches and a highly nervous atmosphere. Ships are far better.

The plane only leaves me as far as London where I get a load of bad manners from a customs man with a bent moustache. He wants to interrogate me a lot, and find out who I am, and what I'm doing, and where I'm going, and when I'll be coming back, and he insists on rooting around in my bag and asking me a lot of questions that I don't want to answer, and he keeps on calling me Paddy like he knew me all his life, and it's very difficult stopping myself from punching him on the nose. "Sure, aren't we all members of the FFF and we can go where we bloody well want to!" says I, but it doesn't have any friendly effect on him. He even gets saucier then and delays me further from wandering around the airport to see how the gaff operates. He only lets me go then when we see on an upside down television on the ceiling that I have ten seconds to catch Flight BFW 3769 to Baulox.

Four

I'm no sooner off the plane in Baulox and feeling confused and looking around for a bar to drown my loneliness for Dublin in, when a lanky man in a brand new suit and silver framed spectacles comes over to me and says, "I am Herr Blumm!"

"Oh are ye?" says I. He looks like he's just stepped out of a razor blade advertisement and very obviously thinks he is tremendously important.

"Herr Murphy I presuppose to understand that the person is you?"

"Hallo," says I, not knowing what to make of the question.

"Very well, thank you, Herr Murphy, for the pleasure of your acquaintance. Did you possess a very interesting and memorable flight?"

"Nah, I don't like whizzing about in the sky."

"You have not wished to be up in the sky at flight?"

"No," says I. And so on. It's like talking to my English teacher, Scut Fagan, at school. Impossible. Then Blumm tells me he is attempting to escort me away to the Kipporster Hotel, or something like that, and we drive off in the longest black car I had ever seen in my life.

There is a bad smell of garlic and sausages in the car, together with a lot of boot polish and dead leather. I'd say the atmosphere would kill a small mouse. Maybe even a fair sized rabbit. I'm hoping it's not going to be a long drive.

"Ireland is a very beautiful country for its excellent view for the visiting tourists," he says, and we drive along all smooth for a while. Then he goes bad bananas! Deliberately attempts to run down a young man who is crossing the street.

"Irresponsibly radical hippies," he says.

"Jesus Christ! You nearly killed the man," says I.

"The City Metropolis of Baulox is problematical sufficient without the radical dangers of hippies and terrorists and hoffsploosh!"

"What?" says I.'

"Oh you will learn proficiency in Baulox in due schedule," he says. It's then I notice the peculiar glazed eyes behind the silver spectacles and just for the laugh I tell him about Dick Muldoon from Dublin.

"Did you ever hear of Dick Muldoon?" says I.

"Thick balloon?" says he.

"Never mind," says I, but I fill him in with some of the details. Dick is one of the best liked characters in Dublin, but Blumm is not impressed.

"Has he not been mentally in the hospital locked away for the good of society and his own welfare?" he says.

"Sure, it would take an army or two to get Dick anywhere near a hospital," says I.

"Or in the prison securely curtailed behind walls," he suggests almost hopefully.

"Not at all," says I. "Dick is free as a bird, and he's the head of the FUA." He looks at me funny-like when I tell him this and goes off into a prolonged gloom. I never met a millionaire before, but I would have thought that what with all the loot in the bank and having eight or nine cottages in Cork and Kerry, and a very big factory in Baulox to boot that he'd be laughing all the time.

But he isn't laughing at all. He's deadly serious with a face as long as a giraffe's neck.

Five

And his face gets longer by the minute.

(By the way, if you're wondering about Dick Muldoon – Dick is the head of the FU All Movement in Dublin and he's on permanent protest and uproar. He protests mainly about solicitors, shopkeepers, publicans, policemen, priests, politicians, farmers, bishops, bureaucrats, and people like that. The other people love him.)

Blumm seems to think that a man like Muldoon is a very serious threat to a stable democracy, whatever that is, and he doesn't want to hear any more about the man. If a person tried to do anything like that in Baulox he would immediately be "Gasztflumbackornookt" and (whatever that is) that would be the "very end of the matter."

We drive on in silence to the Kipporster Hotel where I'm glad to see Blumm is in a terrifying hurry to get on about his work. One of his employees from the Works would collect me in the morning. That he thinks is a "Gomsteiner arrangement" and "hoping that everything is in order to my own personal satisfaction" he drives away in his long car. I hang around the hotel for about ten seconds and go out for a look at the city. It's not like Dublin at all. All the streets are straight and not so much as a sweetwrapper blows along the pavement. Nobody stands around on the corners singing ballads and selling newspapers. I don't like it.

I goof around for a while and get back to bed about three in the morning where I immediately fall into a bad nightmare. Me and Blumm are together in a long black rocket heading off to somewhere I don't want to go, and the smell of garlic on board is ferocious. At the same time the cleaner woman from the hotel is tugging at my shoulder and roaring her head off. Incongruous is what the da would call a situation like that, and to make matters worse she is gabbing away in a foreign language. "Herr Flarsky!" she keeps shouting, together with a lot of other nonsense. I only wish she'd get herself lost.

"Herr Flarsky! Herr Flarsky seben unterfluster vilk um daggon," she roars. And it's only then I remember Blumm's man from the Works.

"Alright, alright," says I getting out of bed, and I go upstairs to see what all the fuss is about. It's your man alright that Blumm sent to collect me — a small stout fellah with lots of noisy toothless laughs. He shakes my hand, all the time spluttering out jokes, all in Baulox not a word of which I can understand, and out we go then to a long black van, his arm around my shoulder like we are long lost brothers, and soon we are pissing up the Baulox Highway on our way to the Works.

Six

Have you ever been in a Russian mental asylum run by absolute lunatics who keep all the very sane people locked up? No? Neither have I , but that's what the Works remind me of – something horribly weird that shouldn't be on this planet. Now, Scut Fagan my famous English teacher will tell you that my descriptive passages are a horrible eyesore and that in forty years of teaching he never came across a worser brat, but I suppose you could say the Works are like a congregation of dirty grey boxes and oily pipes spewing this way and that, and heaps of metal cluttered together any old way, and the whole contraption surrounded by high barbed wire fences with a moxy of armed guards mouching about the perimeters. A terrible looking kip!

It's like driving into a war zone after somebody has blown up the world. Flarsky isn't so ha-ha funny with these lads with the guns, only laughing the once and cutting the cackle immediately when they fail to catch the joke. However, when they wave us into the parking compound he goes at it again, making up insufferable jokes and roaring out of himself like a prolonged elephant fart. Then he switches off his engine when we're parked outside a big metal pipe, turns to me, big grin and very delighted with himself, and says, "Ah! Garzorkheitenschlott!"

"What?" says I.

"Garzorkheitenschlott!" grinning like the monkey when it started raining bananas, and pointing around at the ghastly grey buildings.

"Oh Jazus!" says I. It's obvious now that the word means home. Can you imagine?

And can you imagine me and Flarsky trotting through a big black steel door with the words "GOOB STANK!" and a big red skull with an X under it, painted on it, and then on single-filed into a narrow metal cattle chute where we are searched by three uniformed gunmen. I can just imagine Jody and the lads dossing around Dublin having a great white whale of a time, and I'm feeling sorry for myself.

And it's not a cattle chute – it's some sort of security gadget and it goes very bad bananas when I get to the end of it. Lights and bells go off and a pandemonium breaks out as more gunmen appear from everywhere shouting and waving guns at us. Later they calm themselves down a bit when Flarsky shows them a very official letter, and they pin a small plastic disc on my jacket, just like the one Flarsky wears only mine is PV 689735927 xhe.

They wave us through as if we were going somewhere important, and on we go down a long narrow corridor, Flarsky still chucklehooting all over the gaff until we stop outside a grey door. Flarsky straightens his tie and knocks.

He knocks again. Then again. Then somebody inside says "Hoofbam!" and we go in. It's a small office with a large desk and a short fat man behind it with the exact same type of spectacles as Herr Blumm pretending to be studying something on his desk. After a while he looks up startled, as if he hadn't heard us coming in, gets himself up and comes over to us, big smile and about three times as many teeth as he should have.

"Ah ha!" he says. "Herr Paddy Murphy from Irelander, how very exquisite it is to be meeting with you. I am Herr Zuckermutter, director of everything personal. . ." Very soon he is talking complete absolutely unimaginable mumbo-jumbo.

"And you have understood exactly what I inform for you?"

"No, I haven't the foggiest," says I. That flummoxes him for a while but it doesn't take long before he starts yapping again.

"Hostereichernokloatonhobbel stugg! And now we all three immediately tour around sightseeing all over the Works and examine the beautiful view. Ha! Ha! You must be very agreeable?"

"I suppose so," says I.

"Your English of Irelander is very strange to my ear and not being my custom when I was in Oxford."

"Do they speak like that over there?"

"Exactly very precise to the minute detail."

"Good for them!" says I.

"And before we depart one question to be asked before we lead you on an excursion – work you have already undertaken before in a factory I have understood?"

"Yea, I worked in a beet factory in Bristol but it was nothing like this gaff."

"Ah ha! Beef factory! Excellent choice. Different to what we are here. Yes?"

"Yea, nothing like this place at all."

17

"Yet similarity in all largesque factories, beef, automobile, fertilpisers, all largesque factories. We have director of everything personal, high level security, bluggerworkers, white collars, blue collars. . . So now we must tour off!"

And off we go, Zuckermutter in the lead, Flarsky breathing down his neck, and me trailing at the rear. Up and down and around and in and out. The place is chockerblocker full of warehouses and weird machines that must be robots that go around on their own. . . birp. . . birp. . . birp. . . and people with serious faces. Very intense! And all I want to do is go back to bed and maybe to dream a bit. After galloping around for an hour or so we end up really pissed off with each other's company in Q-Sector in Basement 45 which I understand is to be my place of work. Then Zuckermutter and Flarsky leave me in the company of six men and a robot, and they skiddaddle off about their business.

Now for the impossible task of describing Q-Sector and the men in it. Of course, six years with my English teacher Scut Fagan learning how to write the life story of an old boot doesn't help, but however.

Can you imagine the guts of a pile of rocket engines and all their complicatory components spewed about on a huge concrete floor, fluorescent lighting, green plastic shelving, steel topped benches, assortments of tools, and six pale faced men in blue nylon workcoats and a purple and yellow robot standing around me like I was a prize goat. And all of them spluttering away in Baulox not a word of which I can understand, and the robot blooping and flashing.

Then the messy business of shaking hands for the second time and further introductions – Herr Ghoulman, Herr Ugidet, Herr Duaditty, Herr Fickling, Herr Windtail, and Herr Purdoppe. And of course Zinky the robot.

Well?

I don't suppose you can imagine all that, but I can, and what's more I can see it vivid as a movie film, with Herr Windtail, the mean faced man with the stoop, wagging a crooked finger at me and indicating that he wants me to follow him somewhere.

I don't want to follow him anywhere – I've had a bellyful of it already – but I obediently go down with him to the darkest end of the basement where all the oily junk is. He immediately gets stuck into this muck and starts piling it up neatly on the shelves along the wall. Then he points at me, points at the filthy junk on the floor, and points at the green shelves. I haven't a clue what he's implicating, and I'm not too sure I want to find out.

"Daf blugger duk dein rafters histooch," he says.

"What in the name of Jazus are you saying?" says I. We stand there for a while definitely not understanding one another. And then he gets what the da calls the base effrontery to pick up a dirty metal object which looks like a giant penis with a hook on it, and hands it to me.

"Very interesting!" says I, making sure to put it straight back on the floor where it belongs.

"Nack! Nack!" he says. He takes the gadget up off the floor again, slow and methodical, and carries it over to the shelf. Then he picks up an identical looking object and tries to hand this to me. Naturally I don't want any of them so I shove my hands in my pockets and shake my head.

Seven

What a fucking lunatic! Windtail boils over and goes deep purple in the
face and shouting out of himself like a drunk at a hurling match. I don't
know what to make of the situation at all. And his eyes – they start
rolling around bonkers in their sockets trying to escape out of his head,
but lucky enough the teabreak hooter blasts off then, and he relaxes
himself a little. We go up to join the others for Coko and sausages. That
I think is the end of the farce, but doesn't he go rotten bananas again a
few seconds later, nearly choking himself on a sausage, spluttering pork
and phlegm all over the table, shouting and pointing at me and generally
breaking out in a bad rash. Over he comes to me straight after the break,
wanting me to go back with him to the dark end of the basement. He has
his glue, and I make it quite clear that I'm not going anywhere with him.
And doesn't he go lunatic juice again.

"Gaztjerktein puus!" he roars.

"Ah go and jerk yourself," is all I can think of saying. And at that his
body loses control of itself, shakes itself into an apopletic dance, and his
long arms go waving about in the air looking highly dangerous. I just
don't want to hear any more about it. I've a feeling I'd like to get the
blazes out of there, hightail it back to Dublin, meet up with Jody and the
lads and forget I ever came to Baulox. And I'm just about to walk
straight out of there when Windtail suddenly screams, "Goofter Garter
Gott Splocht!" and storms off on his own. What a relief! With him out
of the way I get a chance to look around to see if there is anything useful
to do. First off, I go over and do an examination of Zinky the robot. He's
operating in a corner out of sight of the others, picking up bits of metal
and walking around in circles.

"Hallo, Zinky," says I but he says nothing. He looks so miserable
that I feel sorry for him. They have him wandering around aimlessly
picking up bits of machinery and dropping them off in a heap beside the
doorway. He's a strange looking creature – square purple head with
yellow and black eyes, long legs and arms and big rubber wheels under
him. Naturally I'm wondering can I get him to do something a bit more

sensible but the trouble is that although he seems to understand Baulox he seems bleeding impervious to simple English.

"Stop acting the prick, Zinky," says I but on he goes. . . birp. . . birp. . . birp, picks up more machinery, walks around in a circle, drops it, and does the same trick all over again. There's a sort of typewriter gadget on his backside which seems to me the best way of finding out how he works. I try punching 999 to see how that affects him but he just acts stupid then – waggles his hips and splutters. I try 888. Not much result. 777, and doesn't he have a nervous breakdown. I never saw anything like it: bloody lunatic robot picks up a metal bar and nearly brains me. He then goes off at seven hundred miles an hour, and creeps up behind Herr Ugidet who is welding metal frames together.

Herr Ugidet is a tough-faced bullet-nosed midget with one eye missing that was probably blown out in a war. He is seriously concentrating on his welding and doesn't notice that Zinky is standing behind him and about to knock his block off with a heavy metal club. Obviously the robot was a latent schizophrenic and only waiting for his chance. I think Ugidet is gone for the priest, but he's quick and doesn't seem to want to go exploring into the next life. He ducks just as the metal bar comes crashing down on his welding machine. Zunk! Sparks scutter about in all directions.

"Zinki wast dast dort doobooten!" says Ugidet. (Maybe: What the hell are you at?). Zinky doesn't seem to give a hoot. He begins taking up the metal frames and throwing them about. And soon we're all ducking behind tables and what not to avoid the missiles and the place starts looking like the insides of a bomb explosion in a pig factory. Zinky scores a direct hit on the Coko and sausage machine – sparks and smoke and a very bad smell come streaming out of it. An alarm goes off and to add to the confusion Herr Windtail starts shouting directions and orders in high pitched Baulox. He must have been born in an army barracks square for he wants us to launch a suicidal attack on the robot but lucky enough Zinky blows a fuse. He splutters out a puff of smoke and sits himself down on the floor with a bemused look on his face.

It's a sort of an anticlimax. A doctor is called to have a look at the robot, and two physicists arrive to look over the Coko and sausage machine and things start returning to normal. Because I think it's some of my fault that Ugidet's welding has been messed up I go over and give him a hand. As I said, he's a tough-faced, bullet-nosed midget with one eye that was probably blown out in a war, but apart from that there's nothing really distinctive about him except for the baldiness of his head and the pair of dark goggles that are nearly half as big as his face. At first he doesn't seem to like me watching how he does it and copying his welding technique on the machine beside him. He starts shouting at me and I'm thinking I have another Windtail on my hands until he bursts out laughing. After that it isn't so bad and he even helps me to learn the welding. He shows me a few little tricks and gives me a coloured pair of leather gloves and goggles. By the time the dinner hooter blasts off I'm nearly making the frames as quick as himself and there's good feeling between us. On the way to the Works Cafeteria I'm very much the worker like I haven't been since I worked in the beet factory in Bristol. I'm dirty and sweaty and tired and giving away all my energy to the bosses and working at something I've no interest in and thinking I'm insane not to walk straight out the door.

Eight

Dinner isn't much joy! First you queue up for your chit. Then you queue up for your sausages. Then you wait for your pickled cabbage and then you queue up for your seat. I sit down by the window where there are a few seats where nobody else seems to want to sit. Outside is a high grey wall and fifteen long black vans with "HOOFMACHER" printed on each of them. I'm sitting there not eating anything, staring blankly out the window, trying to avoid the smell of the sausages, and thinking back on Dublin and Jody and the lads. It was at the Christian Brothers school that I first met Jody — they are the half priests and half men (though as the da says it's hard to generalise: some of these Christian Brothers were ten per cent priest and ninety per cent abnormal; others were the other way around; half of them were crazy from not being able to have enough sex, and the rest of them were frustrated saints, oddballs, football maniacs, sadists, thicks and gomdaws. And some of them were just off the wall) who teach us to read and write backwards. Anyway me and Jody sat together in Scut Fagan's class for Latin and English. Normally we got thumped every day for misinterpretation of the books that Scut called classics. He had a thing about these classics which were in reality a load of stuff and nonsense about Julius Caesar, a man who used to live in the old days before they invented English, and plays and stories about kings in England which were alright until Scut explained them to us. He liked to rob all the colour and excitement out of them and beat us up when we couldn't undertand what he was talking about. That was alright until he discovered neither Jody or me knew what an absolute ablative was. Mother of divine mercy! He grabbed a handful of hair out of my head and yanked Jody's ears halfway out of his skull.

Of course at this stage you'll have to understand that Scut's head was too heavy for the long crooked neck that sprouted out from his chalky clothes. He was a bit like a giraffe with an elephant's head on him that talked at a hundred miles an hour. Anyway on that memorable day of the absolute ablative Jody saw red and gave him a hefty dig on the nose to try and straighten his neck and followed up with a well timed left uppercut to the jaw. And me and Jody walked out then leaving him lying on the

23

floor with a big clump of hair in his hand. And we never came back either, although I was sorry in a way because behind it all I liked the lunacy he used to come out with, and the outrageous red remarks he used to write on my essays.

And I'm thinking about all this when a blondey haired woman with overblown boobs comes over and tells me "that management was reserved in advance at the window view and alternative accomodation would have to be located." Of course, I sit there not understanding a single word she's talking about until she gets all red in the face and waddles away with herself. Then three men in brand new suits and silver framed spectacles sit down beside me.

These men are managers. Anybody can see that. They are highly suspicious all the time, darting quick glances to what the others are eating and stopping every ten seconds to glance at their digital watches. It's like they are expecting the restaurant to explode but they aren't quite sure when. I can only guess what they are saying.

"Hockero dooster floost peur dianem fagg!" (Excellent sausages for this time of year!)

"Huk duust harterhodd?" (What about the cabbage?)

"Jep intermazzion harterhodd goafer shittdoorst." (I think the cabbage is an international disgrace.)

Or something like that. Obviously not talking about what the da calls important matters pretaining to the spirit. I never had dinner with managers before. And I never will again if I can help it.

Nine

Herr Blumm arrives down to Q-Sector immediately after the dinner and
everyone starts pretending they are about three or four times busier than
they were before. He comes straight over to me and Herr Ugidet, and I
think he's a bit surprised to see me welding.

"Your father has the information withheld from me as to your
qualifications as a welding operator."

"There's nothing to it."

"H'mm. . . My reason for my whereabouts this distance from my
administrative office in the Administration Building is for you to be
informed (gooftar!) that satisfactory accomodation has been located for
your convenience at Flustorf Street which I trust you will find strictly in
order to your personal satisfaction. This very evening on the termination
of the day's work Herr Flarsky will collect the company vehicle
(Hornega!) for to escort you to your new lodgings. (Gooftar!)
Tomorrow morning you must discover your own method of arrival at
work. Promptly we begin work at eight o'clock sharply on the dot and
all our employees are punctually efficient. (Tistroff!) I have discovered it
to be a fact that punctuality is not the custom diligently carried out in
Ireland, ha! ha!"

"No. I seldom surface before ten or eleven."

"On the surface, you. .?"

"I usually don't get up too early."

"You must adapt your habit, yes?"

"I suppose so," says I.

"Tray Behan! I am pleased for you to settle so perfunctorily at your
work. (Oh Bunsk!) I have nearly forgot. I am to understand that your
standard of proficiency at Baulox is the cause of a misunderstanding
having taken place in the Dining and Recreational Halls, so we have
undergone the task of enrolling you in the Serbski Institute For
Modermask Baulox where you will be thoroughly Bauloxized. . ."

"I'll be what?" says I.

"You will learn how to speak our language. Herr Flarsky will detail
you with the arrangements."

25

"Okay, fair enough."

"Bumbowl!"

"What?"

"Bumbowl! As you say in your country, goodbye until the next time we arrive together. Herr Flarsky will escort you on my instructions at precisely five o'clock."

"Okay, good luck."

"Bumbowl, Herr Murphy!" he says and strides away leaving me wondering what he was talking about. And it gives me something to think about while I'm working.

Herr Flarsky bombs into Q-Sector just after the five o'clock hooter blasts off and a few minutes later we are safely installed in a long black van and pissing back down the Baulox Highway after an uneventful day at the Works.

If he's not laughing he's grinning all the way to the Kipporster Hotel where he turns serious when I insist on sitting down for a bite to eat. He gets his grin back again, however, when I order for two and a couple of bottles of wine as well. Seeing as Blumm is footing the bill and a millionaire more than three times, I may as well. And sure soon I am even laughing at Flarsky's jokes myself. (Dist hooten margon par ab dunkstein hokegelt, ha! ha!)

After a few bottles of plonk I gather by the few words of Baulox I'm picking up and Flarsky's exquisite sign language that he is going to show me the town. And there is no stopping him either. Before we have even left the hotel he is making very obscene gestures about the places he is going to take me. And soon the manager and waiters are acting very suspicious and hovering around our table like they might have served us up some poisonous wine.

Now before we go rushing off into the night, take yourself a gawk at the detailed map on page three so that you won't be getting all confused by the different parts of the city. Baulox is divided into two sections – East Baulox and West Baulox. The East is sort of a respectable dump with a lot of houses, hypermarkets, and neat little gardens, but the West is a different kettle of fish altogether. There you have the Casinos, Fun Parlours, Wank Centres, and the Flesh Clubs and thousands of perverts from miles around hanging about trying to enjoy themselves too much. Flarsky of course has no idea of putting in the night in the East – he beetles straight over the Baulox Flyover into the West Sector and pulls up outside a place called Scuntza Taverna Nite Club. Big red and yellow neon lights outside and photographs of women in the raw.

In we go, Flarsky doling out a pile of money at the door. It's very dark inside and I can't see much except shadows in the neon lights at one end, and a curved bar right out of a television space saucer advertisement at the other. Flarsky marches us straight to the bar and orders a couple of drinks. Obviously he knows the place very well. He turns around to two unhappy looking gougers who are leaning against the counter and says, "Dab Suck Fluchers marstafft, ach sie jaxdunkt flurt donk!" and breaks into a loud howl of laughing. I'm wondering how the two men will react and it doesn't take long to find out. One of the gougers casually turns around and smashes his beer bottle across Flarsky's head. Flarsky stands there dazed for a few seconds with an uncomprehending look on his face, but he has a tough nut – without blinking a lid he picks up his own bottle and thumps it across the gouger's nose who screams and collapses to the floor. His mate moves in with a broken bottle and I have to pick up the heavy glass ashtray and brain him with it. Then things start getting completely out of hand. Heavies move in on top of us from all angles. Two of us against seven or eight of them. We haven't a chance. I see a clutter of bluish white lights and wake up in an alleyway outside with a bleeding and anxious Flarsky kneeling at my side trying to get me to my feet. I moan and attempt to get up but just then the Baulox Army arrives.

As the da says, I'm a little naive at times. I'm thinking that these soldiers have come to our rescue, and I keep on thinking that until a big black boot with a steel cap comes crashing into my face.

Ten

One boot follows after another. It's a real sickener, and all I can do is turn my face to the ground and try to shield my head with my hands. Things go hazy. We are shoved into the back of a lorry. Flarsky moans away on the floor beside me and someone puts out a cigarette on my arse.

Later they haul us out again and into a barracks. They beat us up again. I don't know where we are. There is a red light overhead. They ask questions. They keep on asking questions. Flarsky is taken away to another room. More questions. Who are you? Why are you causing a riot in a respectable nightclub? What terrorist organisation do you belong to? I just want to fall asleep but they won't let me. I wonder does the anonymous looking man behind the desk ever sleep. He looks freshfaced and clean. I'm filthy and feel like a mistreated dog.

"What is your name?" he asks again as arrogant as ever, and in the back of my head I hear the voice of my hurling coach Jessie McGrath — "Don't give in Murphy! Don't give in until you bleeding drop!"

"What?" says I.

"What is your name?"

"Haven't you got my passport?"

"You must answer all questions from a to zee. Otherwise we will arrive nowhere and we have all night. It is for your own benefit."

"But they don't make sense. I've told about six people my name already and I'm not going to tell you again."

"Kluski!"

Again the young soldier with the long blond hair punches me in the stomach. Out goes a mouthful of blood and phlegm I had been saving and it lands on the bridge of his nose. He hits me again.

"Kluski! Garnst nokt!" says the man behind the desk. Kluski restrains himself.

"Now we must be very reasonable. You must tell me your real name," he says in his monotone accent. It's funny, he looks such a harmless little guy. He'd pass as a shopkeeper or a clerk in the Registry of Mortgages.

"Ah go and piss yourself!" says I.

"Kluski!"

This time he digs his knuckles in under my ribs and it hurts real bad. I gasp and fall to the carpet pretending to faint. Whatever else happens I am going to get this blond bastard. As I'm lying there he slaps my face. I pretend not to notice as my wind comes back. I'm thinking if only he would move over a little within the range of my left boot. I raise myself groggily to my feet all the time trying to manoeuvre into an attacking position but Kluski keeps moving to my side. And just then the telephone rings. I can scarcely believe it. Kluski glances away from me at the sound on the desk.

I pull my left leg back slowly and deliberately, and as Kluski turns around to face me again, I plant a ferocious boot in the seat of his balls. He sags to the floor with an astonished whelp and I turn to the man behind the desk who has dropped the phone receiver and is reaching for his gun. His nose snaps in a splatter of blood as my fist connects and he goes tumbling off the chair and whacks his head a wallop off the radiator. There is no fight in him at all and he passes out cold.

Then I take up the black rubber truncheon from the desk and beat the living daylights out of these two thugs. They offer no resistance at all. Bad bastards! When I'm satisfied that they're nearly dead, I pocket my passport and money, and as an afterthought I take their two wallets, the sheaf of papers in the filing basket, the truncheon and the gun, put them all in the brown briefcase, and climb out the window into the laneway outside.

Eleven

The laneway is very dark and I'm not sure which way to go. And all of a sudden I'm shivering goose pimples and vomiting. Ugh! I ate too much at the Kipporster Hotel. I want to sit down and maybe sleep but I have to get out of there. Low grey buildings stretch out on either side of me. I try the left where there are less lights.

I'm walking up that way with my briefcase trying to look like a business executive who happened to have strayed into the barracks in the dark and don't I hear a chorus of wojeous screams. It's like someone is castrating a herd of baby pigs with a breadknife. It must be the political section. I'm thinking if I had a bomb I'd know what to do with it, but I don't so I change my mind and head back the other direction.

I pass the window I escaped out of and the screams sort of fade out and instead I hear a lot of men singing, "Duf monktrappt keizer kommfuckt plooger plizer yo!yo!yo!"

Then I hear a brass band winding up and loud clapping and more yo-yo-yo!s. It almost sounds worse than the screams at the castration cere-monies but I don't stop to find out what's going on. I hurry across a carpark to a sort of a crossroads and see a gate down to my left in the big wall. It's closed and there is a sentry in a little glass box reading a newspaper. I'm glad he can't see me because he has a machine gun. I creep down behind the hut to the wall and isn't the first thing I see a metal stairway leading up to a sort of observation platform on top of the wall. I climb up this and jump down onto the street outside. As I go on my ear on the pavement I can hear my hurling coach Jessie McGrath — his voice is ringing in my ears: "Well done, Murphy!" he is saying. "You escaped!"

I'm on a narrow street at the edge of the West Sector. Lucky enough there are rakes of whores patrolling the pavement so nobody notices me, an executive on his way home after a late night at the office. I head in what I think is the general direction of the Kipporster Hotel. Halfway there I come upon a pub with an English name, The Harbour Bar. Doesn't make sense to me because there is no river or harbour or anything like that, but I decide I'm in need of a drink so I go in.

It's a curious pub. Looks more like a toyshop than anything else on the inside. Model aeroplanes and trains and all sorts of junk on wheels all over the place, on the shelves, walls and floor. A man with long grey hair and bushy sideburns is fiddling about with an electric train set on the bar counter. There is nobody else there except for seven or eight drunks who are sitting mesmeric in the corner. Obviously out of their skulls.

"Anyone speak English?" says I.

"Yes, I have an excellent English," he says.

"Is there a barman about?"

"Yes, I am the proprietor," he says.

"The what?" says I.

"The owner," says he. A real cool customer. Doesn't even bother to look up from the model railway set.

"I need a drink," says I.

"You need a hospital," says he looking up at my face for the first time. And I see what he means when I glance into the mirror behind him – I look like an old man of about twenty-five and there's blood all over me. Makes me look tough.

"I'll be alright," says I. I was a lot worse after the hurling match against the Belmullet Rangers.

"You came over from the West Sector?"

"Yea, I got beaten up over there by the army."

"Yes, it can be a dangerous place for a young foreigner. Wait there and I'll fetch my wife."

"Lola!" he shouts up the narrow stairs at the back of the bar. And then he introduces me to the drunks.

"They were all in the Resistance!" he says, and the whole group of them look up and grin at me in unison.

"The Resistance?"

"Oh, you are too young perhaps to remember," and he doesn't say any more because his missus arrives on the scene. She's a slender woman with sad blue eyes and short black hair. She takes to me immediately, fusses over me like a nurse, and puts bandages on my face. She is very interested in Ireland, tells me the husband and herself spent four years in Blascore An Craith (the place where the gate blew off its hinge) in County Tipperary. She also tells me Baulox is no place for a young Irish lad like myself and if I had any sense I'd get the hell out of it on the next plane. I agree with her.

She calls herself Frau Echolle and her husband Mister Echolle who she tells me was a big figure in the Resistance, whatever that was. He wants to know if I'm interested in model railways.

"No," says I, "I haven't the slightest interest," and I have to pay for my drink then. The drunks in the corner are highly interested in model railways because that's how they get all the free booze. When his missus goes back upstairs I ask him is there anywhere I could rent a room.

"It might be possible," he says.

"Where?" says I.

"We rent out rooms ourselves at times."

"I've come to the right place then," says I.

"Twenty-four Kacks a month plus electricity," he says.

"I'll take it," says I. It sounds fairly cheap especially because I have two walletfulls in my briefcase which were probably stuffed with bribes and prisoners' money. One of the first things the soldiers had done was take Flarsky's money.

"Lola!" Again he shouts up the stairs and his missus comes running down again. He tells her they have a new paying guest and the rent will go toward getting a model of the Rio Grande Express Train, and she shows me to a small room on the second floor.

"You'll be happy here," she says.

"I hope so," says I, wasting no time getting into the bed and falling into another nightmare.

Twelve

I think there are twenty-seven soldiers after me. I'm in a narrow side street hiding behind a garbage container. They want me dead because I have the secret or at least they think I have. What it is I don't know although I think it's got to do with a new formula for garlic sausage. They are closing in on top of me. Suddenly a bomb goes off and an ambulance roars by. And I wake up to find Missus Echolle sitting on the bed beside me.

"Seven o'clock," she says.

"Auaugh God!" says I, stretching and rubbing my eyes.

"You must be awake for work," she says.

"Oh mama!" says I, sitting up on the bed with a lot of bad memories coming back at me. It's amazing how a few drinks takes the good humour out of an early morning and I'm wondering are the soldiers out searching for me.

I get out of bed with a terrible headache and a pair of rubbery legs like I was after playing a hurling match. I'd have to go and tell Blumm I wanted out of there on the next flight to Dublin. While I'm zipping up my fly Missus Echolle rants away about coffee and pancakes. You'd swear she was holding a party and I have to duck out the door of the kitchen when her back is turned and hurry along the side streets to the bus terminus at the edge of the Baulox Highway. There are hundreds of people there getting ready to go to work. I try to ask a few of them which bus to take but they keep backing away from me as if I was trying to steal their morning newspapers.

I haven't a clue which bus to take so I stand in the shortest queue and within seconds I'm on board bus 583 wiping the wet fuzz off the window so that I can look out. Nearly every bus I had seen pull out motored up the Highway in the direction of the Works. Bus 583 is the exception. It shoots across the road onto the overpass and bombs into the West Sector.

Oh shit! It's one of those days. Then the driver gets nasty when I tell him I want to hop out at a set of blue traffic lights. Finally he lets me out about two miles down the road outside an early morning cafe.

"Shagg!" he says mysteriously before he takes off again.

"And shag you!" says I going into the cafe. Several workmen are inside sitting around circular plastic-topped tables playing cards and drinking large glasses of purple wine. Seems a bit strange to me at that hour of the morning. I sort of guess they are night workers.

"A coffee please," says I to an enormously fat woman who is reading a beauty magazine behind the counter.

"Shagg ba mornoff kopt," she says.

"Hallo," says I.

"Shagg ba marnoff kipstucht," she says.

"Just give us a cup of coffee," says I. I'm in no humour for a big pile of complicated Baulox. "Coffee," says I again and doesn't she hand me a glass of purple wine. I give her a five Kack note and she gives me back four Kacks and ninety-five Pimpernells. It's cheap stuff.

Tastes like diesel oil with a dash of cough mixture but after four glasses of the stuff I feel like a new man. I'm going to bite the head off Herr Blumm when I get to the Works.

"Shagg!" says I, ordering a fifth. I'm getting in on the trick now and some of the workmen are winking at me.

"Funk Pimpernolla," she says and I give her one of the plastic coins and take the drink over to the tables to watch the men playing cards. It's a game for five players. Each player gets thirty-seven cards. The object of the game is to capture all your opponents' cards, drink as much shagg as possible and win the money in the centre of the table. This is done by roaring your head off every five seconds, piling Pimpernells onto the table at the most unexpected times and grabbing wildly at any cards you see lying around. For some reason I don't understand the short man with the castrated moustache wins all the money and one hell of an argument breaks out.

"Bas kupt Pimpernolla dus en fuchen swiezer!" they all roar and reluctantly he puts the Pimpernells back into the kitty. And everybody bursts out laughing including myself. A ridiculous game altogether. But great fun!

Thirteen

It's after one o'clock by the time I get to the Works. I had decided meanwhile that it was Blumm's job to get me safely back to Ireland. It wasn't my fault that Flarsky had cracked a load of bad jokes and I had to defend myself against the thugs in the Baulox army.

I'm hardly inside the security chute at the front gate when I'm cornered by seven gunmen, all of them wanting to stick the nozzles of their machine guns in my ribs. They argue a lot amongst each other but after a while they escort me to the very place I want to go – Blumm's office, which is a big glass bubble at the very top of the Administration Block.

What a ghastly view! Outside, a contortion of cement and pipes twists for miles in every direction, factories spew steam and smoke, and over to the West is a huge blob of land covered in snot. I don't know what they were trying to make but I couldn't even have invented such a scene in one of my nightmares.

"Now, Herr Murphy, please place yourself in a seat," says Blumm and dismisses his gunmen with a wave. I sit down on one of the enormous puffy armchairs. Blumm is sitting in front of me behind a horrible wooden desk from centuries ago that he must have stolen off somebody's great grandfather. On the desk are three yellow and three pink telephones and on the glass wall behind him is the craziest stupid looking painting I've ever seen with a lot of pink balls on it.

"Now, Herr Murphy," he says. "You are aware that yesterday evening at five o'clock precisely instructions have been passed to Herr Flarsky from me to escort you to satisfactory accomodation in Flustorf Street which we have undergone the trouble and expense to arrange. Gooftar! This has transpired not to have taken place. Tistroff? That we must understand."

"Yea, I know," says I.

"So you must inform me as to exactly what has transpired to happen."

"What happened was, we were beaten up by the Baulox army."

"Kaskram! Where has this event taken to a place?"

35

"Outside Scuntza Taverna."

"So! Hooftor Schnott! Herr Flarsky has reprimanded my orders and has escorted you to an establishment of irreparable reputation. Shart? Why?"

"We just went out for a couple of drinks."

"When was the last hour you were with Herr Flarsky?"

"The last I seen of him he was getting his head kicked in by the soldiers in the barracks. It's only a wonder they didn't murder the man."

"A most unfortunate manner of placing your words, Herr Murphy. At one o'clock this exact morning on the dot Herr Flarsky was released by the army. Berstrig! Very much later his corpse was discovered to be dead floating over the Swurge River."

"Oh Christ, they murdered the man. Bastards!"

"Whom did you say has murdered?"

"The army murdered him."

"Now, Herr Murphy, I must warn you immediately that such a possibility is an inconceivability. Figuratively and unimaginable and a falsehood."

"Of course they murdered him. D'ye think they'd let him go after I escaped? Sure, they would have killed me as well if I hadn't got out over the wall."

Blumm quits talking for a while. He's highly nervous about something and keeps tapping his silver pen on the desk. I can't think of what's wrong with him unless he has ants in his pants or his doctor's pills are having side effects. Finally he picks up one of the yellow telephones and speaks a hundred miles an hour into it. Then he sits back in his chair, removes his spectacles and smiles at me. He has about eight gold teeth up front.

"Please relax, Herr Murphy, my secretary Manda will bring Coko. Klorkor! I see we will not conclude this affair in matters of seconds."

"Okay," says I, but I don't feel like relaxing at all. They're after murdering Flarsky for cracking a bad joke. And no doubt Kluski and his superiors wouldn't mind doing me in as well. I don't like the situation at all and Blumm's gold teeth don't help. I wonder how Jody would've handled the situation. And I'm wondering about this when Blumm's secretary comes in like she just stepped out of the centre pages of the *Daily Slit*. She's tall, with long black hair, and I can see through the short blue dress she's wearing. She doesn't bother with the knickers.

"White nudder black, Herr Murphy?" she says.

"What?"

"Your Coko."

"Oh yea, thanks."

"That all for now, Manda," says Blumm, and she goes out leaving a heavy stink of perfume behind her. Me and Blumm are left facing each other over cups of Coko. It's what the artists used to call surreal in the old days before they invented robots. A glass dome. Gold teeth shining over a cup of steaming Coko. A weird view. And nothing ordinary in sight. And I'm asking myself what the hell I'm doing here.

"Your father is what we call a highly astute man," says Herr Blumm.

"A what?" says I.

"He is highly astute. He did warn me about what you say – your blegertite."

"My what?"

"Your overheated temperament is the correct word, is it not?"

"I don't know," says I. Jazus, he has a much bigger amount of words than myself but uses a peculiar way of stringing them together. Scut Fagan and himself would have a powerful conversation if they ever got together.

"Your father has me well informed for your intuition of discovering trouble."

"You can't blame me, I didn't start anything."

"Now, Herr Murphy, we are not dividing blame. This is a serious situation and what we cannot allow is a varp weilschnagger. . . a deterioration to develop. Can you reach agreement with that?"

"Yea, sure."

"Very good! Then first and foremost you must attend an interview with the army."

"No way," says I.

"I can assure you, Herr Murphy, for you to cooperate with this interview is a mere formality. I do not admit to holding pride with myself about my attributes of personality, however I do admit to being in the Metropolis of Baulox to pull tightly at the important strings."

"Cooperate with what?"

"You are aware, Herr Murphy, that we have utmost problems at this time in the State with insane terrorists so it is of vital importance that the army maintains vigilance at all times. Unfortunately slight mishaps may happen infrequently."

"I wouldn't call that slight. Murdering a man like that for nothing. Just 'cause he liked to laugh."

"Now, Herr Murphy, I am very much older than you are so I have the heavy experience of years. Did you know that when I was young what you are now, I had not two Pimpernolla to rub together, and you just have to peep out this window at what I have slowly built up over the years. In other words I can assure you that we must maintain discretion. The army has it on good authority that you seriously assaulted two of its officers for which offence you could securely be locked away for fifteen or twenty years. However this very morning I have been in conversation with Juckstein Blude, the chief commanding officer of the West Baulox Army, and it is understood between us that the army will take a lenient overlook of the situation if certain insurances are undertaken by you. Gimellstraff?"

"What do I have to do?"

"He has informed me that Kernoff will receive a quiet transfer of the two soldiers in question if you maintain discretion."

"You mean if I keep my mouth shut?"

"Precisely. We must not embarass the army in these times of difficulty. Gimellstroffer?"

"Yea, okay, if it'll save my own skin, I'll keep my mouth shut. Where did you say the two gunmen were going?"

"Gunmen?"

"The two soldiers."

"The two officers in question will be transfered to Kernoff to patrol the Nitric Acid Plant."

"Good enough for them — bad bastards. I hope they drown in the stuff."

"Putting it in another way, Herr Murphy, you will have no further trouble from them. Gimellstroffer?"

"Yea, okay."

With that said he gets onto another of his phones and talks a load of very important sounding Baulox down the line. I notice my own name cropping up now and again. When he puts the receiver back, he shows off his gold teeth to me again and tells me a man called Herr Krimp would escort me immediately to army headquarters. And afterwards he would escort me to my new lodgings on Flustorf Street. I would be allowed the rest of the afternoon off work, and this time Blumm says there will be "no Goonschluffer!"

Fourteen

HERR KRIMP TURNS OUT TO BE A THIN NERVOUS SORT OF CHARACTER WHO SPEAKS ENGLISH IN A PECULIAR WAY LIKE AN ENGLISHMAN. HE EVEN PRONOUNCES HIS HAITCHES WHEN THERE IS NO SENSE OR NEED. AND HE'S VERY STRAIGHTLACED AND SERIOUS. NOT LIKE FLARSKY AT ALL WHO I'M GETTING WORRIED ABOUT FOR SELLING HIM DOWN THE RIVER. MAYBE HE HAS A WIFE AND FAMILY THAT ARE GOING TO BE VERY WORRIED ABOUT NOT BEING ABLE TO HEAR ANY MORE OF HIS JOKES. HE WASN'T A BAD SKIN AT ALL AND MAYBE I SHOULD DO SOMETHING ABOUT IT. BUT WHAT? WRITE TO DICK MULDOON IN DUBLIN? HE'D SOON SORT THEM OUT! ASK JODY FOR ADVICE?

"What does Goonschluffer mean?" I ask Krimp a few minutes later as we are driving out of the Works in one of the long black vans.

"There is no equivalent word in English, my good man," he says.

"It must mean something," says I.

"Goonschluffer," he says, "is what you say to a child when he is being naughty and deserves a good spanking on the bottom."

"It means no messing," says I.

"H'mm, not exactly, my good man."

"Oh it doesn't matter," says I. I've lost interest at this stage and I'm thinking about Flarsky. When the man you were with the night before is suddenly murdered it creates a vacuum. And life seems to lose a lot of its meaning. It's just crazy.

"Tell me," says I, "did you know Herr Flarsky at all?"

"I have met him briefly. However, in all my time at the Works we did not strike up an acquaintance. I am afraid Herr Flarsky is a little vulgar for my tastes and for the life of me I could never unravel the man's sense of humour."

"Did you know he was murdered last night?"

"Please! Keep these opinions to yourself. Officially he was blind drunk and fell into the river."

"That's a cover-up job."

"I'm not a detective, my good man. May we let the matter rest?"

"I suppose so if you don't want to know. . ."

"It is of no business of mine. And if I might advise you, you should make it no business of yours."

"Yea, that's what Blumm seems to think as well. . . Are we near this kip yet?"

"This kip?"

"Army Headquarters?"

"We are almost there," he says glancing at his watch, "and I daresay we should arrive in perfectly good time."

As I might have guessed, Army Headquarters turns out to be the biggest and ugliest building in the whole of Baulox. It's a colossal blob of concrete with dark black windows in the centre of a huge compound. Around this runs electric fencing and alongside to the right is the barracks that I think I escaped out of. As we drive in the gateway we are surrounded by a swarm of gunmen. Most of them are armed to the teeth and trying to ask two questions at the same time. Krimp is as cool as a fish in water.

"Hortz huffcant hubber?" one of the gunmen shouts.

"Hortz guft organiztmostrukkenschneider?" shouts another like a bust up cement mixer.

"Veben vust Herr Gluglob getzstraffen," says Krimp calmly.

"What are they on about?" asks I.

"They are merely establishing our identities."

"Well come on, let's get out of here if they don't want us to go in."

"No, no, Herr Murphy, we must be patient with these matters of protocol."

It's a difficult place to get into. We are ordered from the car, interrogated, locked in a small steel box, scanned, x-rayed, screened, put through a security chute, searched and in my opinion abused, so by the time I sit down in front of Herr Gluglob in his office on the tenth floor I don't really expect to get out of there alive. But then to my surprise Gluglob turns out to be halfways decent.

"How do you like the City of Baulox?" are his first words.

"It's a grand place altogether," says I.

"So you like it here?"

"It's a lovely city," says I.

"And you'd like to live and work here?"

"Nothing more I'd like."

"Very good. All we want to do is for you to answer a few questions and sign a routine form and you may go then."

"Okay," says I, pretending not to be too relieved.

"Your date of birth?"

"It's there on my passport. . . thirteen, the seven, and one."

"That would make you seventeen, is that right?"

"Yea."

"Now to the more awkward business — how did you escape from the Hickphart army barracks last night?"

"I got out the window."

"And what about the two officers who were guarding you, or were supposed to be?"

"They got very violent, fighting with each other, then one of them collapsed off his chair and hit his head against the heater, so I just took my things and left."

Gluglob seems to think this explanation is funny in some way but I make sure to keep a serious face.

"So you escaped out the window and afterwards met up with your companion Dunter Flarsky who had been released by the army?"

"No, I never seen him again after I got out."

"We have a report here from a reliable source which says Herr Flarsky was seen with a tall foreigner fitting your description at four o'clock in the vicinity of the Swurge River."

"Ah no, I was with my landlady at that time."

"And her name?"

"Couldn't spell it for you — something like Missus Hooley."

"Frau Hoofmacher?"

"Yea, something like that."

"I see. Well, that's all we want to know. We shall be making further discreet enquiries. Now, if you sign this statement I think we may let you go. A slight misunderstanding all around."

"But that's in Baulox, I can't even read it."

"I can assure you it's merely routine."

"Well get Herr Krimp to translate it for me."

"Brambi, hudder mort gestop dikim hollim."

Brambi, the short flat faced gunman, goes out and fetches in Herr Krimp who translates the document.

BAULOX BAIL RELEASE SHEET NUMBER SEVENTY-EIGHT THOUSAND AND SIX HUNDRED AND THIRTY-TWO.

I, Paddy Murphy of Thirteen Flustorf Street Baulox 34 make solemn oath and declare:

ONE. On the night of Tenth August last I was acting in a drunk and riotous manner outside Scuntza Taverna in the West Sector in the company of one Duntar Flarsky.

TWO. In the company of said aforementioned Duntar Flarsky I resisted lawful arrest and to wit assaulted Putto Milch, Fruck Harnstein and Ghustov Varneke, officers of the 69th Brigade of the West Baulox Army.

THREE. The said Duntar Flarsky and I were taken into custody at the Hickphart Barracks and subsequently released at one a.m.

FOUR. I have no complaints to make regarding the treatment Duntar Flarsky or I received while in custody.

SIGNED . . . .

DATE . . . .

WITNESSED BY . . . .

"Ah, I couldn't sign that," says I, "that's a pack of lies."

"Very well, Herr Murphy. Brambi nonto dukstein naket tobo trieben."

Brambi shows Krimp the door again and I see Gluglob isn't so friendly after all.

"Garnster nucht!" he hisses through his teeth.

"What?"

"You have given us no choice in the matter. We must now bring you before the Criminal Tribunal."

"Why?"

"To answer charges of drunkenness, assault, larceny and murder."

"Murder?"

"Yes."

"Ah, come off it, I didn't murder anyone."

"That is for the Tribunal to say."

"Alright, let's get it over with. Where is this tribunal?"

"I am afraid it will be a matter of several months before your trial, maybe even a year, and in the meantime you will be detained in custody."

"What about bail?"

"You do not understand, Herr Murphy. This is a stable democracy. There is no bail allowed for terrorist offences. But don't worry, you will receive a fair trial. The Tribunal is an elected body with the interests of the state at heart."

"What about a lawyer?"

"Oh yes, the State will gladly send you a lawyer. Free, he will not cost you a Pimpernolla."

"And if I sign that paper?"

"As I said, you would be in a position to go free. Naturally you are under no compulsion to sign. It is strictly your own decision."

"Have you a pen?"

"Ah ha! Very wise. Now we must ask Kerr Krimp in as a witness."

Fifteen

THEY ACTUALLY LET US GO AND KRIMP AND MYSELF GO FOR A DRINK IN
GIGI'S SALOON AND HE TELLS ME ABOUT HIS SEXUAL PROBLEMS AND WE GO
TO AN OUTRAGEOUS NITECLUB CALLED BUMBALLIMS AND SEE A HIGHLY
ARTISTIC FILM BY MAX FEILBURGER, ONE OF BAULOX'S OUTSTANDING
ARTISTES, AND THE ARMY ARRIVE ON THE SCENE AGAIN.

I can scarcely believe it – they let Krimp and myself out. Naturally I
would have thought they'd have shot one or both of us and dumped us
down the river as an accidental drowning. But they don't. They let us
go, very polite and wishing me a pleasant stay as if I'd only been
imagining what they really were. As soon as we get away from the
general area I ask Krimp would he fancy a drink. The nerves must have
been getting at him as well for he pulls in at the first pub on the right,
Gigi's Saloon. With the time of day that's in it the bar is empty but I see
from the photographs of the belly dancers on the wall that the place
probably hots up at night.

It's funny how a few drinks gets at a man's personality for after his
eighth glass of sour whisky Krimp goes all effusive and tells me about his
problems. These in the main stem from his being what he calls a minority
homosexual liberalist who is denied his natural rights. In other words he
can't find suitable young men to play with. He tells me there are plenty
of oldtimers but these are not suitable to his tastes so he has a lot of
tension building up inside of him. It's like he has something in a bottle
that he has to let out every so often for a bit of air. Or so he says but I
don't really understand what's bothering him.

When he suggests a quick visit to one of the better niteclubs, I say
alright – so long as it's nothing like Scuntza Taverna.

"I wouldn't dream of frequenting such a crude establishment," he
says, and we drive across to the West Sector to Bumballims Club which
he tells me is highly respectable. I suppose tastes vary.

What do you do when you go down a short flight of steps, pass
through a yellow door, and there in front of you on a huge cinerama
screen are two men wanking themselves in a telephone kiosk? Okay, you
might be mistaken so you look around to see where the bar is and you
notice the barman is wearing a woman's G-string. And all over the walls
are horse whips and electrical bananas and stuff. You think you must be

in the wrong place. Then Krimp says, "What will you have, Paddy?" as if we had just walked into The Long Bar on Northeast Earl Street in Dublin.

It wouldn't have been so bad if I had not seen Krimp hand out a thick wad of Kacks to the man at the door to let us in. I felt I'd have to have a drink at least to get our money's worth.

"I'll have a pint of stout," says I. They don't sell stout so I have to settle for a large whisky. We sit over at the bar and take a closer examination of the barman — he's about twenty-five, very puffy in the face from using talcum powder, and he has an outsized penis sticking out of his G-string.

"Why doesn't he put on some clothes?" asks I.

"That is Ivor, an English boy like yourself," says Krimp.

"I'm not English."

"Oh yes, of course, I forgot, you are from Ireland."

"A different place altogether — I should know, I worked in a beetroot factory over there."

"Yet there is a bridge connecting the two countries?"

"Nuts," says I.

"Ivor! Kimtorr! Let me introduce you to a new friend of mine — Paddy Murphy from Ireland."

"Hallo," says I.

"It is very nice to meet you. Hello, Bunny-Bo!" he says to Krimp.

"Bunny-Bo?" says I.

"It is my pet name, Paddy. Rather cute, if I may say so."

"Sounds daft to me."

"Now Paddy, you are jesting of course. Let us take a closer peep at the film. It is highly artistic."

"Artistic?"

"Directed by Max Feilburger, one of Baulox's more outstanding artistes."

"Mac Who?"

"Max Feilburger, director of *Geelschnott*."

The two men leave the telephone kiosk and walk through a doorway. Cut to two waterbeds. On one of the beds are two naked women licking each other's thighs. Cut to a man's fly.

"A beautiful scene! Parfust!"

"Yea?" says I.

"Perhaps, Paddy, you cannot see the intrinsic qualities in his art?"

"No, I can't."

Just then the music starts up and Krimp wants me to dance with him. Okay, says I but he turns out to be a lousy dancer. While I'm trying to have a good time jumping about on the floor primitive style, he's all the time trying to get smoochy and paw me. I have to keep pushing him away.

The trouble comes unexpected. In between dances a fat elderly man wearing a woman's dirndl like my grandmother's comes over to me and starts talking Baulox. That's alright until he puts his hand down between my legs and starts feeling my balls.

I stand there for about five seconds unable to believe my goggles before I slowly draw my fist back and hit him a ferocious wallop to the chin. He makes a whinnying type noise and falls to the floor like a snagged cabbage. I didn't mean to hit him so hard and I'm about to help him to his feet when three leather-clad toughs appear out of the shadows and attack us. Poor Krimp! One dig on the nose and he's spreadeagled. I get one of them alright and I'm yanking another by the hair when someone, I don't know who, goes at me from behind with a metal pipe. Again I see shooting stars.

It's almost a repeat of the performance the night before, only this time it's me kneeling on the pavement trying to awaken Krimp. Then I can't help but notice two grey army vans screeching around the corner of the street.

I abandon Krimp and run for my life.

Sixteen

That's another contrarious thing about the da – he seldom panics
himself out of control when the chips are down. I remember the first day
we went out in the sailing boat he built. He had never sailed a boat before
so he sat at the back smoking his pipe and reading the instruction
manual. As it was fairly stormy weather it was no surprise to me that
soon we had turned over and were drifting onto the Dublin Bay Reefs off
Dollymount Strand.

I thought we'd both be drowned. I couldn't see how we'd any
chance at all until the da asked me, calm as could be, would I kindly
retrieve his pipe which had slipped out of his gob and was bobbing up
and down at the edge of the sail. After that we seemed to have lashings of
time to get the boat back on its feet which we did by standing on the
lump of wood that the da had stuck down the hole in the centre of the
boat. And then we limped away from the rocks like a pregnant duck.

I'm thinking about this incident as I'm running into a cul-de-sac
alleyway with two soldiers hot on my heels. I'm wondering what the da
would do in a situation like this. And I don't come up with any answers
either so I dive straight through a plate glass window into a factory of
some description. Ugh! The sound of shots makes me all wobbly at the
knees.

Wobbly or not, I get up fast as I can and run down a long corridor
and nearly knock over a man who is fixing a giant lawnmower.

"Oops!" says I, ducking into a doorway where there are two
women putting on make-up, reading beauty magazines, drinking
coffee, chatting and answering the phone – it's amazing how they can
do half a dozen things at the one time.

"Ger makt gooseweiner?" one of them asks me but I don't stop to
answer. I run out the other side of the office, down three steps, across a
warehouse chockerblock full of lawnmowers, out through a green door,
across a car park, and down the street. Behind me I hear shots and
women screaming.

The soldiers must have gone lunatic juice in the lawnmower factory when they didn't get their man and shot most of the workers. They don't come after me.

I make my way slowly and nervously back to The Harbour Bar in the East Sector.

"Not again!" Mister Echolle exclaims when he sees me. He goes straight to the stairway and calls for his missus. I see in the mirror that I've cut my face somehow and that some of the drunks in the corner are highly amused.

"What's the matter?" says I.

"Vir slukter toftin!" one of them says and Mister Echolle explains that they were in the Resistance whatever that was.

"The Resistance?" says I.

"Oh you are too young to remember the war."

"What war? There's always a war on somewhere or another," says I and forget all about it when Missus Echolle comes down and puts a few more bandages on my face. I try to have a drink then but I'm so shivery that I have to go to bed where I fall into a beautiful dream with the da and myself in a boat sailing across the widest ocean in the world. The only problem is the da has forgotten to fix the hole on the bottom of the boat so I have to keep my foot on it all the time. For some reason I don't want to tell him about it. He's so happy sitting back with his pipe admiring the sharks and the icebergs.

Seventeen

Once more I wake up to find Missus Echolle on my bed ranting about pancakes and coffee and telling me I had nightmares.

"It was a pleasant dream," says I.

"But you were screaming in the night and saying the ship was sinking. . ."

"Ah no, there was nothing wrong with the boat. We were sailing away grand until you woke me up."

"It is seven o'clock. This morning you must have breakfast before work."

"No, I couldn't eat nothing at this hour. Have to go in and see the boss about something."

This time I get Bus 794 and arrive at the Works before eight o'clock with most of the other workers. There are long queues at all the security chutes. I join one of these but again the gunmen single me out for some reason and escort me up to the big glass bubble to meet Herr Blumm. Nothing much has changed except that the view looks even worse early in the morning, and the painting with the pink balls makes me feel I'm imagining everything. Maybe I'm still asleep and dreaming.

Blumm has grown a wart on his nose overnight, and he's irritable – doesn't seem too pleased to see me.

"Gusto Morg!" he says abruptly.

"What?" says I.

"Good morning, Herr Murphy."

"Oh, hello."

"Now we will have much explaining at hand to decipher."

"How do you mean?"

"Herr Murphy, I am quickly losing impatience with this long drawn out affair. You are perfectly aware that yesterday my instructions have been passed to Herr Krimp to escort you personally to satisfactory accomodation in Flustorf Street. Gooftereimo! Machenschlafterpuntz! This has transpired not to happen. Tistroff? Exactly what has transpired to happen?"

"We just went out for a couple of drinks. There's no law against that, is there?"

"Garter gooftereimo hoppellgott! Vas plakt? I must take more attention to your father's words."

"What did the da say?"

"He has sufficiently warned me about your blegertite. Tistroff?"

"What?" Obviously he's getting so excited he doesn't know if it's English or Baulox he talking.

"Never we mind. Hoofterkuffenghoosh! This exact morning we discover an exact event similar to yesterday morning."

"Oh Christ! Did they murder Krimp as well?"

"Garter gooftereimo hoppellgott machenschlefterpuntz! You must handle your words with more discretion! Herr Krimp has been securely detained and charged with very serious terrorist offences against the State."

"You must be joking. Krimp wouldn't know how to terrorise a goldfish."

"My information is to hand that Herr Krimp together with a description of you personally attacked a prominent West Baulox politician."

"Nonsense. . . Oh, you mean the guy wearing the monocle and the woman's pyjamas! I'll tell you what happened – the guy came over to me and started putting his hand down my pants. . . like that. So I gave him a good thump for himself."

It's funny, but when I explained that to Blumm he seemed to relax himself a bit. Although God knows why.

"H'mm. . . interesting – Herr Goobenschlifter verst uftoken sexualistickimo. . . I have wondered was his disposition suitable for the job."

"What job?"

"Never we mind, just private conjectures. Perhaps, Herr Murphy, under these circumstances you may proceed directly with your work. I shall be in a position to handle any further embarrassment and now. . . I must tell you I have a personal obligation with your father so this very evening I shall escort you myself personally to Flustorf Street."

"Alright."

"Bumbowl, my secretary Manda will show you out."

His secretary has bought herself a pair of knickers and as she takes me down in the lift she breathes liquorice allsorts into my face.

"You like it here?" she asks.

"It's fantastic," says I.

"We have an exciting night life here and some wonderful niteclubs."

"Telling you," says I, "Were you ever in Bumballims?"

"Oh, you do get around quick. Bumballims! Quite exclusive!"

"Fantastic," says I.

"Have you been to Zuckweiders?"

"No. Where's that?"

"On the corner of Bladdatukka Street and Flitzen."

"Any good?"

"Fabulous. Maybe I'll see you there sometime."

"Sure," says I, "how about tonight?"

"No, I do not mean it that way. Perhaps we may encounter each other."

"Sure," says I. "What time will you be there?"

"No, no, I cannot go there this night."

"Tomorrow then."

"No, tomorrow I must bring Tabbyticklers to the veterinary surgeon."

"Oh, you've a dog have you?"

"Tabbyticklers is a Manx kitten."

"Oh, I wouldn't worry about an old cat. . ."

We have been walking a fair bit at this stage and I'm beginning to notice the Works is even a weirder place than I had thought. There are robots all over the place and in one building we pass I see several guys running about in plastic suits dipping huge ladles into big vats.

"What the Jazus are they doing?" says I.

"Oh, them! They are only Deb Flustees. Imported labour who volunteer for all the high risk jobs to enjoy a very low standard of living."

"You mean they get paid less?"

"Yes, it is mutually beneficial." I cannot see how or why but I don't ask her any more about them. In another warehouse we pass the workmen who are busy packing large shiny steel gadgets into wooden crates. They look a lot to me like the ground-to-air missiles I had seen live in the Arab wars on television. That gets me asking her what was going on in the Works. She looks surprised when I ask her that.

"You mean you do not know that the Works is A Daf Boomstimmerung Hockmeister Ducksfloosh Plant?"

"A what?"

"We manufacture Ducksfloosh components."

"Components for what?"

"We manufacture components for practically everything, ships, aircraft, hospital. . ."

"Oh, I see," says I seeing nothing, "and what are those yokes?"

"Yokes?"

"Those things," says I pointing to the missiles.

"They are Classified Ducksfloosh."

"Classified for what?"

"You must know it is against company policy for the employees to know the exact nature of the Ducksfloosh."

"But how can they make the bloody Ducksflodder if they don't know what they are?"

"We have excellent instruction manuals."

"I see, well I'll see you tonight," says I. We've arrived at Q-Sector.

"No, I cannot tonight."

"Well, good luck then."

"Bumbowl, Herr Murphy."

"Bumbowl, me arse," says I.

"Pardon?"

"Don't worry, it's an expression we use at home. See you," says I, turning in to face Herr Windtail and his cronies.

Eighteen

I DON'T FEEL MUCH LIKE WORKING SO I FIDDLE AROUND FOR A WHILE AND LATER GET SIDETRACKED INTO WRITING A SHORT LETTER TO THE DA.

Q-Sector hasn't changed much since I was last there. There's still a bad smell in the place – sort of like suffocating rubber in a bath of sulphuric acid with a lot of sweat thrown in. And the fluorescent lights making the workers look like ghosts. And Zinky the robot bleeping and blooping and back on his old stupid job going around in circles picking up scrap iron. I don't think I'll ever be able to describe it properly – Windtail giving me a smelly look as I come in the door. He's still down in the dark end messing around with the oily junk. I don't think he likes me. He sort of snarls and hisses at me all the time pretending he's not looking at me and watching me all the time.

I've half a mind to try and sort out the robot again – he's going to have another nervous attack if somebody doesn't give him something more exciting to do. A man could nearly do what he is doing so there doesn't seem to be any point having an intelligent robot on the job. But I don't like the idea of Windtail thinking I might have caused Zinky's last nervous breakdown, so I just go over to my workbench and get set up for a bit of welding.

My workmate Ugidet, who you probably know by now is the tough-faced bullet-nosed midget with one eye missing that was probably blown out in a war although you couldn't know for sure because he wears a pair of goggles half as big as himself, says nothing to me, just nods his head and goes on with his work. I stick a few metal frames together and then stop because I'm not in the humour. I'm not in the humour for anything really and start doodling about on a piece of paper. It's almost by accident that I get stuck into a letter to the da:

> THE WORKS
> BAULOX HIGHWAYS.
> BAULOX S-28-23J

Hello da,

I suppose you expect this is one of your blasted clients yet. . .

I don't like this letter so I tear it up and start another one.

THE WORKS
BAULOX HIGHWAYS.
BAULOX S-28-23J

Hallo, good morning, about half nine here in Baulox, Paddy
on the blower, letting you know I managed to arrive here in
one piece, but it's not at all like Jody had me thinking. For
starters I thought it would have been an ordinary enough
gaff like Dublin or Bristol but not at all – it's a city for
lunatics, madmen, nuts, mo-mo's, yobs. Yea, it's an
absolute dump. It's bad fucking rotten bananas.

The city is split up the middle by the Baulox Highway
into two halves – the East Sector and the West Sector. In
the morning all the traffic except Bus 583 pisses up the
Highway to the Gump at the top where they've located all
the monster factories including this one. Then all day
nobody does anything except work, work, work like as if
they're thinking it's necessary. Then in the evening the
traffic turns about and pisses back down the Highway again
to the bottom where it swings East or West.

If the traffic swings West over the Baulox Flyover it
brings you straight into a blue pornographic treble-X-rated
horror for adults over the top only – You thought Baggot
Street back in Dublin was bad and going to the dogs! Jazus!
Wait and you see this kip – Flesh Clubs, Pervo Centres,
Fun Parlours, whores and pimps and wankers all over the
place and a crowd of gougers roaming around the streets
with machine guns who call themselves the Official West
Baulox Army. They've already beaten me up, shot at me,
murdered a workmate of mine called Flarsky, put cigarettes
out on my arse, maybe murdered another workmate of mine
called Krimp, and made me sign very important official
documents that were covered with lies. That's the West for
you.

As for the East – that's where you do your sleeping and

eating and watering your flowers and pretending everything in the garden is rosy and nothing at all is going on in the world. There are one or two places like that out on the Southside in Dublin. A strange place. Loads of houses, symmetrical lines, rows of gardens, plastic fishbowls, and artificial designs from the old days and hypermarkets, but it's not much crack to live or even walk there. You'd be arrested for pissing on the street even if you had to, or even for throwing a chocolate sweet wrapper on the pavement. Jayzuzz! And you should look at all the smoke and the soot in the sky and the police roaming around like dogs sniffing out toffee wrappers. Bad as the West is if I'm out for the night that's where I go.

By the way – hardly anyone over here understands plain Dublin English. Mainly it's all Baulox over here and impossible to know what they're on about. And when they do try and get wired into the English no ideas come out of them – it's all mumbo jumbo horrible hodge splodge stuff with twenty-five time too many big long words in a simple sentence. Ye know! Even if I ask someone where is the jax? – that's beyond them. The toilet. Oh! The water closet where you may find a rest room is for private usage of the management only in these circumstances. Jayzuzzz! You should have warned me about that!

I'm on the job at the moment down in a stuffy basement called Sector Q and supposed to be welding metal rods into square frames with a man called Herr Ugidet, but I'm not – I'm writing a letter to you. Ugidet the bloke I work with is not the worst although he gets highly cranky at times and irritable up his nose because he spends most of his money on the Baulox Football Pools and because he never wins anything he has to work harder and harder all the time so that he'll get a bonus. At first I thought he didn't care less about anything but I was wrong because when the robot tried to clobber him from behind with a metal bar he was out of the way like a light. He obviously knows more about what's going on than you'd think.

The job is alright I suppose and I've had three jobs now counting the two boring weeks I spent with you working in the Registry of Mortgages after they kicked me and Jody out of school. I'd rate it about the same as the job I had in Bristol putting the beetroots into tin cans only I'm expecting to get paid more here. I get paid at the end of the month which seems daft to me to wait that long to get your wages.

Did you know that this place is called Boomstimmerung Ducksfloosh factory or something like that. The names they have for things here is a laughing gas! In other words it's a component factory only nobody knows what the components are for because they're classified. And if you ask me they could be making missiles or something like that – the things with the bad heads on them that blow up aeroplanes and cities. I mean, for fuck's sake if they were making spare parts for washing machines they'd probably tell you what they were for. Wouldn't they?

Nothing much else to write home about except I was thinking about our sailing days together and was hoping if I sent you over a few Kacks you might buy another boat. But, seeing how the one you built the last time fell to pieces the first time we crashed it into a bollard, I think it would be better if you got one that was already built. Money isn't much of a problem because I got a load of it off two soldiers who beat me up and have gone off to Karpoff or Jurkstott or somewhere to guard an Acid Plant.

And so be it! Ugidet is beginning to look over this way possibly wondering what all the writing is about, and a nutcase called Windtail is starting over this way so I'd better say good luck for now and get back to work. If you see Jody and the lads tell them the women and the crack are ninety-nine over here and I'm out on the piss every night of the week.

And tell Granda I was asking for him.
Love,
Paddy.

Nineteen

BLUMM PICKS ME UP IN HIS LONG BLACK CAR AND DRIVES ME TO DAF TANK ON THE CORNER OF FLUSTORF STREET WHERE WE HEAR "DAST FUMPTAR STOONK", NUMBER ONE IN THE BAULOX HIT PARADE, BUT FIRST A FEW WORDS ABOUT THE GRANDA.

I suppose now that I've mentioned the granda in my letter to the da I'd better for the sake of immortality and what have you give you a further run down on him. He's what Jody calls a laughing gas ticket.

If you ever go down Black Pudding Lane, past the train station, turn down past the bent metal pole where the kids play hookio and in through the hole in the wall and across the small vegetable garden with the burnt out Morris Minor and into the pub on the corner, you'll find the granda on the stool in front of the cash register with a tweed cap on his head, and if you buy him four or five pints there's a chance he'll tell you what happened in 1916. The granda's da who is my greatgranda was there himself and if you're inclined to believe granda, his da shot more British blackguards and blew up twice as many telephone boxes as the rest of them put together. And if he hadn't had a gammy leg and died on his way to catch the last race at the Phoenix Park he'd be still out there creating One Hell Of A Ruckus.

And I'm inclined to believe granda myself but enough about that for the minute. Blumm picks me up straight after work and takes me away in his long black car out through his own personal gate and glides down the Baulox Highway.

"A high inconvenience," he keeps on saying and nothing else at all and I'm sitting there choking from the stench of raw leather and parched for a drink. I'm thinking of asking him would he fancy stopping off somewhere for a drink only I don't want to put it into his head that it was me that led Flarsky and Herr Krimp astray. I was always having that trouble at school before they kicked me out – teachers accusing me in the wrong of leading people arseways. But it's a strain thinking all the time what other people are thinking about and trying to figure out what they'll think next if you do this that and the other. As Jody says – let them think what they bleeding well want.

"Fancy stopping for a drink, Mister Blumm?" says I, and you won't believe this — Blumm actually laughs! Imagine! And for about one tenth of a second the frozen glint goes out of his eyes.

"Where is this lounge you suggest?" he asks, shining his gold teeth at me.

"Anywhere at all — I suppose we'd better stay in the East Sector."

"Well, in that instance I am very delighted to have a quick drink for your company. It so transpires to happen that there is a small lounge situated at the very corner of Flustorf Street."

"Okay," says I.

Daf Tank is the pub he's talking about and unlike Blumm says it is a monstrosity in size, almost as big as Croke Park but there is no way I'm going to let him know it's the biggest pub I have ever seen in my life.

"This looks fine," says I trying to keep a straight face. We have to walk almost one hundred yards across the floor to get anywhere near the bar, and midway there I get the fright of my life when the resident brass band I hadn't noticed bursts into action. Thundering Jazus! What a sound! They are playing "Dast Fumptar Stoonk", number one in the Baulox Hit Parade. Sounds like they're trying to start a new world war. We have to roar our heads off to hear one another.

"What'll you have?" I shout at Blumm's left ear.

"Vas pupt?"

"Drink! What'll you drink?"

"Oh, no, no, blumtok! I insist on my prerogative."

"Okay, I'll have a brandy and shagg," says I.

"Tray Behan! Vooster fernstein!" he shouts at the barman and waves his pig leather wallet.

After a few glasses of brandy and shagg he springs a surprise at me.

"We might discover for you a vacancy in our Sales Force," he says.

"Sales Force?" says I.

"I am taking notice of your adept mannerisms practised in lounges."

"What do you mean?"

"You can as we say catch the barman's attention without having to speak forthrightly."

"Most Irishmen can do that."

"H'mm. . ." He continues on about his blessed Sales Force. Very boring stuff and not fit for consumption in a bar. I only hope he'll clam up.

"It can be a very useful asset in serious sales negotiations with the Arabs," he says.

"Arabs?" I don't know what he's talking about.

"Let me place it alternatively. During negotiations with Arabs who are as we say Korkwagt. . ."

"Cork?"

"Korkwagt as you say have arrived under the influence of imbibing large quantities of alcohol. . . It can be a very useful asset."

"Sure, the only thing I ever sold in my life was my bicycle."

"Ah ha! Daf Boofshitter!"

"The what?"

"Daf Boofshitter, the bicylce which you will come to learn is feminine. . ."

"Yea. . . And fifteen quid was all Jody would give me for it."

"Jopy?"

"Jody. . . And then he wanted a loan of a fiver."

"Five Boofshitters. . ."

". . .Just to buy me a drink. Ye know? Clinch the deal, luck money and all that sort of jazz. . ."

"Too sufficient amount of alcohol on a Boofshitter is. . ."

". . .And sure by the time we got back from the pub. . ."

"Ah ha! Daf Glitterakker!"

"The what?" Jazus! It's very difficult to tell this guy a story.

"Daf Glitterakker! The lounge! We all come back to the lounge! ha! ha!"

"Yea, sure. . . and by the time we got back from the pub the only difference was that Jody owned the bike and I didn't."

"H'mm. . . And who at the present partition of time holds the ownership in possession of the Boofshitter?"

"Oh. . . the bicycle. The da has the bike — he uses it to cycle to work."

"Gomtray nokt! That is very good negotiations!"

"Yea?"

"Gimmellstroffer schlokterpizzimo! Parfust!"

"So you want me to flog your components to a load of piss-eyed Arabs — is that the story? Sell them a few missiles when they're out of their heads?"

"Garter Hochstrein Gott! Herr Murphy! You will have to discover absolute more discretion with your words in a public situation." He shuts up after that about his Sales Force and begins to look very unhappy within himself. And he doesn't get any happier. What a miserable fish to be boozing with — he nearly gets a seizure when I order another drink behind his back and he gulps it down like it was medicine. He's very itchy to go so we have to leave then and glide around a corner in his long black car and up a short hill to number thirteen Flustorf Street, the house of Herr and Missus Grimmwoof.

Twenty

A SHORT STAY WITH THE GRIMMWOOFS WHERE I HEAR AN UNKNOWN WOMAN IS TRYING TO GET IN TOUCH WITH ME WHO HAS SOMETHING TO DO WITH THE HIJACKING OF AN AIRPORT AND A GROUP CALLED THE LLL. IT ALL STARTS OFF FAIRLY BORING BUT THINGS HOT UP A BIT.

The Grimmwoofs live in a three-storey house with a basement below and a tiny garden out front which sports a pygmy apple tree and two castrated rose bushes. Missus Grimmwoof arrives out to the front door and immediately goes into a tizzy of excitement when she sees us. She's a short stocky woman in a large red and white butcher's apron and while she squeaks out of herself in a loud voice she waves a plastic broom and dustpan about in the air. And she's giving out loud welcoming laughs and walloping me on the back of the head like I was her idiot grandson just back from the moon. As for her husband Mister Grimmwoof, he's like a fly in a spider's web all the time buzzing around at her side and doing everything she tells him to do. He translates some of her Baulox into English: "Very good, Herr Blumm, we expect everything will be to our young guest's approval."

"Excellent," says Blumm.

"Vastarupta gutz flitkorr strachon mitzenhoober!" screams Missus Grimmwoof getting herself into a frenzy again. Blumm does what any reasonable man would do and gets lost.

"Bumbowl!" he says and I follow the couple up the concrete steps into the house. There's a surprise waiting for me in the hallway: Mister Grimmwoof takes a letter from the walking-stick rack and hands it to me. Inside is a note asking me to phone a woman called Zi whom I never heard of in my life.

"Who sent this?" I ask.

"I do not know. It arrived this morning in the mail."

"Flumpid dokentootropp," says Missus Grimmwoof and we follow her further into the house. Ugh! There's a ferocious smell of wasp- and woodworm-killer inside. We traipse up the stairs along the narrow red carpet to the first landing, and after that it's wall-to-wall lino all the way to the top where they show me into a tiny attic room. And I'm standing there wondering why the hell I'm there staring at a lot of holy pictures on the wall. I don't like the implications. Jesus going up a hill on one wall, Moses coming down on another and a blue and white Virgin Mary with her baby sitting on a dirty grey cloud surrounded by a gang of angels playing trumpets. . . and an x-ray photograph of a saint with a huge heart and that's only half of them. Then there's a big black cross hanging over a narrow bed.

"Did a monk live in here?" says I.

"An vunk horboff donk herbfein gootslaften?" he asks his wife and mother of Jazus doesn't she explode into an apoplexy of Baulox.

"Gritterschneidinduffintagertgaftpuptladger dustenteimer shloss mochtorgenn!!"

"Yea?" says I.

"My wife says that our previous lodger was recommended as being of exemplary character but he became immoral."

"I mean, what are all the. . . pictures doing on the wall? Do they. . ." and I can't say much more because the missus is shouting out of her like a football commentator. Mister Grimmwoof has a lot of translating to do to keep up with her.

"My wife says that in usual circumstances we do not take in lodgers but she is a personal friend and relation of Herr Zuckermutter. . .

"My wife says they play bridge together once a fortnight. No gambling of course. . .

"My wife wishes to know at what time you normally retire to bed at. . ."

"I don't go to bed at any fixed time."

"My wife says that the hall door is always locked every night at ten o'clock and nobody arrives or departs after that hour."

"Tell her to give me a key."

"My wife says there is only one key."

"Tell her to get one cut."

"My wife says it is very confusing to have more than one key and it is impossible because of the burglar alarm and the latch chain. . . The previous lodger invited in female guests."

"Fair play to him. I suppose they prayed together?"

"My wife says you may of course have a visitor during normal hours. . ."

"You mean you're thinking of locking me in here on my own with all those horrible pictures, sure I'd go out of my head!"

"My wife says these pictures have been venerated and blessed and handed down through generations. . . And now my wife wishes to be explicit about the minor matters of rents and deposits, which will be paid eighty-nine Kacks today and on the first date of every following month together with a security deposit of two hundred Kacks which will be returned to you if there are no breakages and all the utility and electricity has been paid in full. . ."

And she's talking away and he's translating away and I'm thinking it's a good job I discovered The Harbour Bar which is a far better place at quarter the rent. I'm thinking I can well do without all these mental hospital arrangements. And I'm getting a pain in my arse listening to her going on and on. "Listen. . ." says I, "tell your wife I'm not interested in staying here."

"My wife says that because you are a friend of Herr Zuckermutter she will allow a discount and that you will now only have to pay eighty Kacks per month which is so reasonable for such a charming apartment in a luxurious residential area where the price of accomodation is going up and up and up. . ."

"No, I'm not interested. Excuse me there, I want to get out the door."

"My wife says that you must remain with an agreement with Herr Zuckermutter, she has only newly laundered the bedclothes."

"Listen, I don't give a hoot what your wife says. Now would you please get out of the doorway so that I can go!" says I, my temper getting hotter by the minute. And then they're spluttering English and Baulox all the way after me down the stairs. And phueue! It's a relief to get out of that lifeless house and into the fresh air although I'm still not together – my heart is shaking itself out of tune a bit like it always does when I get trapped in those situations. In school there was always a lot of that, the Christian Brothers telling me I should lock myself away in monasteries and tell my secrets to the priests, teachers telling me I should do that, this and the other. And then when I told them I didn't want to do any of those things, I didn't want to pray to God, or count rosary beads, or. . . they told me I had to or otherwise they'd bash my brains in. For a second back there I thought Missus Grimmwoof was going to go for me with the broom. I can see the headlines: Irishman mysteriously batters himself to death in Flustorf Street.

To calm my nerves I return to Daf Tank and have myself a few more shaggs and I'm almost forgetting about the letter I got until it falls out of my pocket:

> To/ Paddy Murphy
> Urgent, please call the following number and ask for Zi in connection with the bird seed you ordered.

And I have a big laugh for myself. Daft, that's what it is; bird seed my arse, and Grimmwoof and Baulox in general. I'm then getting fairly bored sitting there on my lonesome listening to the brass band battering out "Dast Fumptar Stoonk" for the eleventh time. For something to do I go over to one of the plastic bubbles and try and phone up about the bird seed.

"Hello," says I after losing about three Kacks trying to make the apparatus work, "can I speak to Zi?" And the woman at the other end of the line before she even tells me who she is, tells me there are two men following me around everywhere I go.

"You must be joking," says I.

"Seriously, so what you have to do is. . ."

"I don't have to do anything. I didn't order any bird seed. Who is that?"

"This is Zi, please listen, Paddy. . . "

"Who are you? I never heard of you. How did you get my name?"

"Never mind, never mind, you must lose the two men and meet me in Pedra's bar in the West Sector tonight."

"What two men? What would anyone be following me around for?"

"I will tell you when we meet."

"And who are you?"

"I am Zi, I am a member of the LLL."

"The who?"

"The LLL. The Live Love Liberate assembly."

"Never heard of youz. Some sort of religion is it?"

"Have you not read the Baulox Press? We have been headlines for the past week."

"I don't read Baulox."

"We have been out at the airport."

"Oh have you. . . wait a minute, are you the crowd that hijacked part of the airport?"

"That's us!" she says proudly.

"And what's that got to do with me?"

"I can say no more over the phone. Can you be in Pedra's by ten o'clock?"

"No."

"We want you to testify against the army."

"I'm not testifying against anyone."

"You would be doing a service for mankind."

"No, I'm not interested," says I putting down the phone. Bananas, I'm thinking as I'm heading for the door, somebody is messing me around with their bird seed. Lunatic juice! I'm wondering have I enough money to buy an air ticket home to Dublin.

It's getting dark outside and I'm feeling suspicious and paranoid going down the street. It's a sort of nasty feeling that two men may be following me and I can't see who they are. I'm looking over my shoulder all the time – nobody! I walk down Schlopp Lane quick as I can and suddenly stop and look into a shop window, feeling like I've seen myself somewhere before in an old American spy movie. Apart from that I can't see anything except the reflection of an old woman tottering past in a pair of Wanko jeans and about fifteen trays of overripe sausages. Jazus! Who would want to be following me anywhere – sure, I'm not going anywhere important. Yet I'm not sure. Why else would the woman tell me that? I break into a run, run down to the end of the street, turn left, and duck in through the park gate on my right. And crash into two hefty men in grey trenchcoats.

"Oops!" says I. I've a feeling because of their dark glasses, the way their hats are pulled down low over their foreheads, the way the collars are twisted up around their necks and the suspicious way they are carrying their violin cases, that they are following somebody.

"Sorry, I didn't mean to bump into you," says I.

"Vas gupt?" says the taller of the two, bending down to pick up his glasses. And the other guy is staring at me in a suspicious way like he might shoot me if he had a gun. I don't wait around for explanations, and quickly backpedal the way I had come, back into Daf Tank, and back into the plastic bubble, to ring Zi and to try and find out what was going on.

Twenty-One

The phone apparatus in Daf Tank gobbles up Kacks and I'm about to lose another one when my two comrades come in. They take a seat over by the rear door and put their violins discreetly under the table. It dawns on me then that perhaps they are only innocent musicians who want to play "Dast Fumptar Stoonk" with the brass band. It's the last tune on earth I want to hear so I put back the phone receiver and leave quietly by the front door.

An aimless walk around the block and down the narrow street takes me to the Kiddenscheitter Taverna, a run of the mill pub with the usual photographs of the naked women eating peanuts and the eight or nine old grumps sitting at the bar in front of the pornovision reading the football coupons. I get myself a brandy and shagg and sit over in the corner beside the bunch of plastic grapes.

And there I'm daydreaming and thinking about nothing much – maybe going home to bed – when the two musicians arrive. A coincidence you might say but I don't like the way they're acting, as if they're hot on the trail of a man who has thrown a rotten tomato at their conductor. I also notice that they seem to make everyone else in the pub fidgety and nervous, even the drunks. They stand out about fifteen miles at the bar because they look like they're only acting normal. As far as I know they haven't the slightest interest in me but just to be sure I wait until they hand over some money to the barman, and then I make a sudden exit. Mama! The musicians don't even touch their drinks or bother about collecting change, they charge out the door after me, and there we are, the three of us looking at one another, waiting for somebody to make a move. At first I'm scared silly, then the whole affair seems to be an embarrassing dream, and only then do I see the funny side of it. Obviously they don't want to harm me, they just want to follow me around like dogs so it strikes me I can take them anywhere I want. I decide to take them on a pub crawl.

Our first stop is the Mutzen Bar and naturally I don't let them have any drinks – as soon as they pay for them I zip out the door. This goes on for a while – the Schlimmburger Palade, the Flupsflappharse and another pub I don't remember the name of — but at Schnotts they seem to run out of cash. The shorter fatter guy with the squashy nose has to borrow a few Kacks off the serious fellah with the cauliflower ears, and this time they're very quick and manage to scuttle down a couple of drinks before I reach the door. I catch them out at a few more pubs but they seem to be getting nasty and quarrelling with each other so I take them on a short stroll along the banks of the Swurge River.

About a mile upstream I come upon a kid's raft and just for the crack I hop on it and paddle it out onto the river. My musical companions who are a safe hundred yards behind me stand there looking fiercely perplexed. A little too perplexed! Because Squashnose reaches into his coat and pulls out a gun. Holy Jazus! For a second in midstream I'm thinking I might join Flarsky in the Deadlands but he doesn't fire and lets me paddle away to safety on the far bank where I wave friendly at them and walk away to the West.

The tall guy is afraid to get his feet damp but I can assure you that Squashnose is no dodo — the fucking eejit dives straight into the river and gets his ammunition all wet and useless. Still, I take no chances and run off fast as I can. And lose them for sure before I look around the backstreets for Pedra's bar.

Twenty-Two

THE ARMY ARRIVE AT PEDRA'S BAR AND I LEARN ABOUT THE DOUBLE PLOY AND THE WORKS OF HEINZROOT GOOFTHORK.

I get a dose of bad memories when I find out that Pedra's bar is only a stone's throw away from Scuntza Taverna – poor old Flarksy, he didn't deserve to be murdered like that and him probably the only comedian in Baulox.

Pedra's is a tiny very crowded pub something like the horror holes where the poets drink in Dublin. Inside is a swarm of young-old people listening to ancient records from donkey's years ago – some band called The Beetles who make a horrible jumping jack sort of noise and shout out the word love every chance they get. Not half as bad, though, as the brass band in Daf Tank.

I have to shufflepush my way through a mob of people to get to the bar, and I'm about to order a drink when a young woman in a green anorak tugs at my sleeve.

"Let go," says I.

"Paddy Murphy?" she says, her big brown eyes questioning me. I guess it must be Zi.

"What's all this about bird seed?"

"That was a blind. . . Now we must leave immediately."

"It was bloody daft!" says I.

"Please will you come with me."

"Hang on, I want to get a drink."

"The army will arrive any second," she says, and that is enough. I forget all about drink and follow her outside where we get into a small blue car. We are no sooner inside when two grey army vans roar around the corner at the other end of the street. They pull up outside Pedra's and six gunmen with stenguns pile out and within seconds they have captured an innocent man.

"Ah no!" says Zi. "They have got Perry."

"Got who?"

"Perry, our telecommunications engineer."

"Your what?"

"Never mind, it does not concern you. Why did you change your mind and come to Pedra's?"

"Just to try and find out what's going on. Maybe you know who's following me."

"The military police," she says.

"Why for Christ's sake?"

"Simple! Because you've a job in the Works they think we'll try and contact you."

"How do you know that?"

"We have our informants. Besides, I went to school with one of the secretaries who works there and she knows all about you."

"Manda?" says I taking a wild guess, and she says nothing but I can see by her eyes that I am right. She went to school with Blumm's secretary! It's a small world. And maybe that's why she thought I was living in Flustorf Street.

"But why did you contact me then if the secret police were hoping you would?"

"You perhaps do not understand radical politics."

"What's that got to do with politics?"

"It's called the double ploy!"

"The double what?" '

"The double ploy – once we are aware that they are aware the danger is neutralized."

"Sounds daft to me."

"It is not daft. The Works is the most strategic plant in this city."

"So what if it's well placed?"

"Whoever controls its workers controls the plant. Surely you know the basic counter-revolutionary theories?"

"Never heard of them."

"Have you not read the works of Heinzroot Goofthark?"

"Never heard of the man."

"Astonishing! You must know he's the greatest urban gorilla strategist since Dookmeister."

"Yea?" says I. It's obvious this Zi woman is fond of dropping the old names but they all sound like foreigners to me. For the laugh I decide to drop a few myself.

"Have you ever heard of Dick Muldoon?" says I.

"No, I must say."

"Well, he's the greatest protester on this side of the moon since Adam."

"You are drunk, Paddy."

"No I'm not," says I.

"Whatever, we must hurry now to meet someone who will explain further to you. You must remember I am not a full member of the LLL. I'm only a messenger boy so to speak."

"How come you speak ordinary English?"

"I lived in Belfast."

"Yea?" says I getting more interested in her. It's hard to say how old she is — maybe my own age or a little beyond that, yet she's too eager and serious for whatever age she is. As the granda might say, she believes in something because she hasn't found out what's wrong with it yet. And for some reason she dresses like a man — anorak, short hair, no make-up and dirty fingernails.

We drive off on a bit of a mystery tour of the city and eventually meet up with a guy called Doppelheizer, a nutcase if I ever met one. I don't know where we are — some sort of small city park at the back of a public toilet under a tree, but I couldn't even be sure of that much because it's fairly dark, and to make matters worse Dopplelopper or whatever his name is, is speaking in whispers.

"Ah come on," says I, "let's go for a drink somewhere. What are we hiding out here for?"

"Shh!" says Dopplebopper. "Let me continue."

"Alright, go on," says I.

"And as we have spoken, you may wish to, not I repeat as a full fledged member but as an auxillary trainee you can be allowed become a member of our organisation," he says.

"But I don't want to join anything," says I.

"So you are here simply to waste our valuable time in this instance," he says. Nasty little official bastard, the sort that always examines your shoes before he gives back your ticket.

"I didn't ask to come here," says I.

"Very well, we shall cease with the interview."

"Suits me," says I and Zi offers to give me a lift back to the city centre. On the way I find out she is very disappointed that I did not join their group and she's hoping I might change my mind. "Maybe you will when you learn the real facts behind what is going on in this city?"

"But myself and Jody and the lads — even Micko who is a revolutionary if there was ever one — we never join anything," says I getting out of the car at the Baulox Bus Station.

"It is for the good of the cause," says she.

"We like to do things our own way," says I.

"You are very immature, Paddy, but I will contact you again — maybe you'll reconsider."

"Yea, okay. Good luck!"

"Vloo videlteimer britzt!"

"What?" says I.

"We shall overcome!"

"Sure. See you!" says I as the blue car darts out from the pavement and disappears around the corner. And once again I'm all lonesome for Dublin or something. It's an empty feeling. For something better to do I make my way to The Harbour Bar. Home, sweet home.

Twenty-Three

LIVING A QUIET LIFE FOR A WHILE, AND ATTENDING THE SERBSKI INSTITUTE FOR MODERMASK BAULOX.

I take it easy for the next few days, working, eating, sleeping; I avoid the West Sector and its niteclubs, and make sure no musicians follow me home to The Harbour Bar. All in all I feel a bit more relaxed about the city but the routine is beginning to get in on me — up at seven, down to the bus depot, work, sausages and Coko, work, sausages and cabbage, work, bus, a special manoeuvre on Kurski Street to avoid being followed, home to The Harbour Bar, a few drinks with Mister Echolle and his drunks — he tells me for the umpteenth time about his model railways and fills me in with more and more details about the Resistance — and then bed.

Things are going alright at the Works, but Zinky blew another fuse when I tried to teach him a few more tricks — scatterbrained robot! He's off at the hospital now getting his head examined. I'm still working with Herr Ugidet, and he's very well although he's losing loads of money on the football coupons. He winks at me now and then with his only eye when he shoves his goggles up on his forehead. I don't have much to do with the others but they all shake hands with me every morning and say gusto mord! Even Herr Windtail, who is suffering from some disease and about to drop dead. I think so anyway — his face is turning redder and redder, boils and pimples are sprouting out on his skin, his hands are always shaking, and he's started drinking on the job yet it's no wonder because he spends all that time down in the darkness with the oily metal trying to stack it on shelves. But he's wasting his time because there is no end to the stuff for whenever he starts clearing a space for himself, Zinky brings down more junk — or at least he does when his head is working. I often wonder why he wanted me to be down there wasting my time as well.

I'm almost relieved when Blumm tells me that they've signed me up for a two week intensive course in the Serbski Institute for Modermask Baulox. This means I get off work early for a while and I think it's a break in the monotony, or at least I think that until I actually arrive there. It's an anonymous looking building over near Army Headquarters with steel walls and little black windows. Inside it looks like an electronics factory converting itself into a mental hospital – what an uproar! There's hundreds of tape recorders, headphones, audi-visi machines, televisions, loudspeakers, all blasting out Baulox at the same time with one or two foreign students like myself listening on. It's amazing with all the machinery and so few students – about four I think, although there's loads of men and women in white coats running around twisting the dials and taking notes.

Of course, I have to start off in the beginners class; they give me a shot of Rezuccio that's meant to help me relax, then screw on some headphones, antennae and electrodes onto my head and shut me into a metal cubicle facing a television screen. Then they switch it on and the lesson starts. Holy Jazus!

With the amount of Baulox coming at me at the one time it's impossible to think, and as for the television, it's on the blink! It's going at twice the speed of light and I can't really see what's showing. Things pop on and then before you can see what they are they pop off again. Craziest stupid school I was ever at, even worse than the Christian Brothers; I can't understand a single word. There must be about eight voices talking to me at once and believe it or not I fall asleep right in the middle of it all. Because I suddenly find myself waking up and everything is silent. The elctricial gear has been removed from my head and one of the women with the white coats is smiling at me.

"Same time tomorrow afternoon, Herr Murphy," she says and it's funny, for a second I find it hard to understand her because she's speaking English. All that Baulox makes your head whirl.

And so it goes on for a few more lessons and one night I find myself leaving the Institute with my mind totally blank. I don't know who I am and I'm wandering along the street going nowhere in particular, not thinking at all, and for some reason I stop a traffic cop on the pavement.

"Durtriff aux hixstalt potte?" says I, and he looks at his watch and says:

"Hort aff fump."

"Gatcha!" says I and continue on down the street. Mama! It's only then I actually realise I had been speaking Baulox. It seems that unbeknown to myself I was learning the language.

I think it's about after my sixth lesson when I meet Zi outside a bookshop on Heilik Street. I'm heading back to The Harbour Bar and my head isn't working right – I mean, I'm trying to think about Jody and the lads in Dublin but for some reason I can't. Everything is fogged up and believe it or not I can't even remember all their names. . . Jody,

Micko — they're easy, you can't forget Jody's brown eyes, and the curly black hair, and the mad stare and the tooth missing out front. Or Micko who is always looking four or five ways at once. . . But the others. . .?

"Paddy!" she says and for a second I don't recognise her.

"Oh how'ye!" says I. "What are ye doing?"

"Waiting on someone. And you?"

"Oh, just goofing around."

"Have you changed your mind about. . .?"

"Oh that?" says I and suddenly I'm a bit nervous because I'm thinking of asking her to come out with me somewhere. I'm getting a bit fed up wandering around the city on my own. If it was Dublin there'd always be Jody or one of the lads.

"Have you?" she says.

"Well. . . I haven't really been thinking about it."

"You should have been!"

"I suppose I should but. . . " says I finding it very hard to think of some reason to ask her out. But to hell with the reasons as Jody always says — "D'ye fancy coming out to the flicks some night?"

"Flicks?"

"Pictures."

"Oh, the movies. But there's nothing showing except bourgeois junk."

"Well I just thought. . ."

"Okay, Paddy, it's a date. When?"

And so we arrange to meet outside Plobkofski's Bookshop, and I pass over another hurdle — it's the first organised date I've ever made. I must be getting old.

"Are you still in the Works?"

"Yea, still at it."

"It's a wonder, Paddy, why you want to work in a place like that."

"It's not much different than working in a beetroot factory."

"A Boomstimmerung Plant manufacturing dast fumptar stoonk, come off it Paddy!"

"Making what?"

"Nuclear bombs; surely, Paddy, you know what you work at."

"Oh," says I, "so that's what we're doing!"

Part Two

Dif Tuber Cultza
(The Middle)

Twenty-Four

It must be two months later when Blumm tells me I must go out and meet his missus. It seems that she has a thing about Ireland and wants me to fill her in on some details.

"My wife has an exorbitant fascination with affairs and events that take place in Ireland historical and retrospective," explains Blumm as we're driving out to his house.

"Yea?" says I.

"So that is the reason she insists on meeting with you so that you may contribute your enlightenment about the current state of events."

"I could tell her a thing or two about Dick Muldoon."

"Muldoon?" says Blumm. Obviously he doesn't remember that I told him about Dick the first day I met him. I don't bother to explain because we've stopped outside a huge museum that's built in the shape of a castle.

"Why are we stopping here?" says I.

"This is my little retreat," says Blumm.

"You live here?" Jazus! He must have a big family or be related to Frankenstein or something: the front garden is as big as the Phoenix Park, and the house itself is as big as the Custom House and the GPO stuck together. In we go and the insides of the place would give you the creeps; there's a horrible loneliness in there and everything is painted up like four centuries ago.

It's one hell of a long night. The three of us sit in huge leather armchairs listening to the big brass clock on the mantelpiece which goes chock-chock-chock and every twenty minutes or so it bursts out into an unholy uproar with bells clanging. Waken the dead it would! And frighten the living to death every time it takes a fit.

Missus Blumm speaks an even more peculiar brand of English than Blumm himself which she says she learnt in Kerry when she was staying in one of their cottages. I could speak better Baulox myself but Zi has taught me a trick she learnt in Belfast of not letting on how much you know. That way you find out that people you think might be friendly are cracking nasty jokes about you in front of your face.

"I have noticed your admiration for our highly valuable antique clock that has been purchased for us as a bargain at nineteen thousand pounds English plus sales tax and transportation costs to this country without one solitary scratch or interference with the excellent mechanisms in its interior."

"Yea, it's a nice clock," says I thinking that the thing isn't worth a wank. I'm also wondering what part of Kerry she used to live in because they didn't speak like that when I was down there at the Fleadh Ceoil.

Then she brings in an old teapot from one of Napoleon's wars and a purple saucer with five skinny dried out biscuits on it. Imagine! Coming home to that with all his loot in the bank. I think Blumm should put his foot down and tell her to make him a couple of sandwiches and stop bloody messing. But he toes the line all the way, and I suppose it'd be bad manners if I said anything about it. The da is always telling me that good manners are the mark of a civilised man so I keep my trap shut.

I don't suppose anybody wants to know what Missus Blumm looks like, but I'd better make a picture of her just so that you'll know what's going on. She looks like a sack of onions.

"These shortcake biscuits are specially manufactured for me by Horner in Paris and are guaranteed to be calorie free and excellent in nutritional values," she says.

"Yea?" says I. The biscuits are like cornflakes – you'd get more food into you by eating the box. She looks like an oversized sack of onions, maybe a few tomatoes thrown in, and all wrapped up in a purple stage curtain. With two black stumps sticking out the bottom of it.

"I always make it a point of policy to order foodstuffs from the most reputable establishments in order to ensure that they are adequate edibly speaking," she says.

"A good idea," says I. Her neck seems to have disappeared altogether although she has three and sometimes four chins.

"Of course we can never be certain at this time and age of the quality of what is being advertised in the common marketplace."

"No, you wouldn't know what you're getting nowadays," says I repeating something granda told me once when he couldn't get a head on his bottle of stout. She has a beakish nose sticking out under the blue-tinted spectacles. And wax-white hair on top with more streaks of blue. An imposing sight, as the da would put it.

"And now," she says, "we come to what must be the highlight of our evening, for as I have noticed in Ireland your people never mention the point of their conversation without invariably long discussions about matters not relating to what they wish to speak of until the conversation is subtly changed in a form of conversational thrust and parry until the exact topic which they wish to converse on is reached. Who was the group of terrorists that was responsible for the blowing up of the Pzintzer Plant in Ireland in current affairs?''

"What?" says I.

"My wife," says Blumm coughing his way into the conversation, "is highly interested in Ireland culturally and historically speaking and has been closely following current affairs in that country for some time now."

"Yea, I know," says I.

"A fascinating country and beautiful for its view," says Missus Blumm. "And I have been studying its history closely from the time of long ago when it broke away physically from the main continent."

"No, that's a myth," says I.

"You mean it was never a segment of the global land mass?"

"No. An island it always was and an island it will always be," says I repeating what Wolfe Tone's grandaughter told to my granda. It's funny the amount of stuff you can learn off your grandfather, especially if he has a few pints under his belt.

"But the geological sciences have determined this fact and further-more that even presently in this day that Ireland is moving at a certain fixed speed out into the Atlantic Ocean."

"Yea?" says I now knowing that she has a screw loose in her head on top of her other qualities. She thinks Ireland is some sort of a boat, although it wouldn't be a bad idea to get further away from England.

"It was the Norsemen who founded Dublin," she says.

"That's a myth too," says I.

"But it has been established that. . ."

"Dublin is as old as the hills. There was always someone there as far back as anyone can remember — sure, the Murphys were there long before Saint Patrick."

"It was he who brought Christianity to save the pagans."

"It was him who destroyed the country entirely. Even James Joyce says that. Before he arrived there were ard ris, ceilidhs, fleadh ceoils and great times to be had by all. He brought the country to its knees."

"Yet the country was inhabited by barbarians and pagans."

"Who told you that?" says I.

"It is the historical fact," says Missus Blumm.

"It's a fact that's all wrong," says I. "Before he arrived the country

79

was full up with musicians and poets and dancers and hurley players. And then his followers brought over about seven or eight King Henrys and you know what they did!''

"Perhaps you will elucidate the matter for my wife," says Herr Blumm.

"There's nothing to relate about it — they just robbed all the land and made up a lot of laws to say that they owned it in the first place. Pack of lies. And then they wouldn't grow anything on it which caused a famine.''

"And this has been written down in your historical books which you have learnt in school?''

"I don't know what was written in them. I learnt my history off Micko and my granda.''

"And what," says Blumm, "is the view on current events in relationship to investment and revitalising of the Irish economy by means of industrialisation by companies from abroad?''

"Well, Micko thinks some of them should be blown off the map, of course he's a bit of a revolutionary like Dick Muldoon. The granda just hasn't any time for them as far as I know.''

"What is the proper surname of Micko that you have mentioned?'' says Missus Blumm.

"What do you want to know that for?'' says I.

"It is my wife's interest in history that prompts this conversation,'' says Blumm.

"Indeed,'' says his Missus.

"But Micko isn't history. Micko's alive and well.''

"Hymmph," says Blumm, and the talk sort of peters out then. His missus complains about a pain in the side of her neck which is peculiar because she hasn't got one. And Blumm drives me to the Baulox Bus Depot. He tells me it was a memorable evening and I sort of sympathise with him for being married to a battleaxe.

Twenty-Five

I'M NO SOONER BACK FROM THE MEMORABLE EVENING AT BLUMM'S WHEN I FIND OUT MISSUS ECHOLLE IS NOT TOO HAPPY ABOUT MY HAVING A GUN IN THE HARBOUR BAR AND THAT LEADS IN A ROUNDABOUT WAY TO DISCOVERING THE EIGHT SANE MEN. IT SEEMS THAT THE EIGHT SANE MEN ARE VERY IMPORTANT PEOPLE IN BAULOX.

As far as I know what happens is Missus Echolle is dusting under my bed and she finds the gun and the papers and the two wallets I borrowed off the West Baulox Army. She doesn't tell Mister Echolle because he has an aversion to guns after having nearly been shot by several of them during the Resistance. Instead she waits for me in my bedroom. When I come in she's sitting on the bed with the gun and all the army papers scattered around her.

"Oh, hallo, Missus Echolle," says I.

"Paddy, I cannot allow guns on the premises."

"Oh yea, I'd forgotten about that."

"But why, pray, is a young man of your age the owner of a gun?"

"It's not mine. I found it, but you can throw it out if you want."

"Yes, I will do that. And the papers?"

"Yea, you can throw them out as well."

"Good, because it is not the right thing to have top secret military documents on the premises."

"Top secret, are they? Maybe you could leave them there and I'll get rid of them later," says I. If they're all that important I want to have a good look at them.

"Okay," she says taking the gun away with her. For a grown up she's a good person — some people would probably have reported me to the police.

I'm left sitting there with the pile of papers and they make very interesting reading because they are all about the activities of the Eight Sane Men.

DUKSPLOTTE MARKOR BRAINSCHOLAPP DA 8 TERRORRISCHE MOSCHEKOLL SAN STADT BAULOX BEIST NAK SIEGUMPERMAGISTRERR MOSK JUSKOR SAN

DIABOLISHET GAN ERSCHNITT BUDDER FLANILLGOT.
DAF 8 MUCHEL MINIZIONIST SAN STATH BEISHT NAK SIE
NARPROK SIE KERNST KAMPTS OST FLUGIONES DARKEN
MURKSTEI NUCLERONEZIONI INDUSTRALT VUSKERAM
AVER DUB FLARKISHT!

It's fascinating stuff: it seems the Baulox Army are in a great hurry to
lock up the Eight Sane Men.

DAV 8 SAN E TERRORIBOK FLUSPART DOOSTERGAASTEN
SCHNOTT IM MARGEN TAMPERSUCKS!

Because the Eight Sane Men are very critical of prominent West
Baulox politicians and are constantly saying things that the army doesn't
like hearing.

H OPPLEHEITER DARVEST SUCHENZOOTER MAP DAR
SCHLAMM DIF ZINTGOGG SAN STADT BAULOX. . .

But the army can't put a finger on them because the Eight Sane Men
are smart – they've given a great heap of embarrassing papers to
important lawyers in Jerusalem and if one of them was to be suddenly
murdered in the army barracks without any explanation there would be a
big commotion kicked up. That happened once before because there
used to be Nine Sane Men and one of them, a certain Bikter Strintinki,
was killed in a plane crash along with 657 innocent passengers and
naturally enough the lawyers in Jerusalem guessed that the Baulox Army
blew up the plane. So they opened their deed boxes and let a few
skeletons come out and such an awful fuss was kicked up that it caused an
unprecedented "Bumsteiner" in the government's administration. Ever

since, the army have been slow to murder any more of them but they are keeping a sharp eye on their activities and probably know more about them than the Sane Men do themselves.

A good way to give a picture of the eight is to translate word for word what the army says about their careers.

1. Hofflart Kartroffe. Bred up in Baulox about sixty-three years back. Knows an awful lot about high powered physics, neurology and sex. A rotten egg and should be put on trial and quietly liquidised at a suitable time in the near future. See Guideline No. 6727. He votes for terrorists in the secret ballot. He causes horrible rows with the overworked government about the "Derb Fluonpishter" and "Dub Gharlarsk" in the nuclear industry. He insists that criminals have the right to air their obnoxious views in public. He activates mobs of people by making long outrageous speeches inciting the brainwashed public to harass the legitimate guardians of law and order. He is a very dangerous perverted man who writes obscene letters to the terrorist presses abroad. He is both on the extreme Left and the extreme Right at the same time and his activities public and private should be monitored by following Procedure ZT 84777.

2. Doctor Ignatius Frippe. A nasty foreigner who emigrated from Persia when he was six months old. He has written "Dukel Doofe Ump Diteshite", which levelled perverse criticisms at the Baulox Government and called them a wojeous crowd of eejits. He later wrote "Dastad Doomp" which is the bible of the breakaway terrorist organization, the LLL. It is rumoured that he fell out with this group because of their "Jarsnort Scutor" (juvenile bunk). He is possibly on the Left and moving Right at a dangerous speed. Procedure ZT 22098519!

3. Stuttkorr Duddhaert. A native Bauloxonion. Expelled from the Baulox University when he was found to be reading subversive literature including the works of Heinzroot Goofthark and books by John Steinbeck. He's a compulsive activist. Never sits down quietly. Always pops up in the wrong places at the wrong time. He incites. He upsets the rabble. He is a dangerous terrorist class 75 B. He makes perpetual lies about government officials including a recent claim that they are not in

the Centre as they always have been since they were democratically elected to preserve law and order. Procedure ZT 84777!

4. Darold Schnapter. 89 years of age. The oldest Sane Man in Baulox. A homosexual vegetarian and terrorist. Has been inciting riots since he was thirteen. Always causing the government embarrassment. He has a bee in his bonnet about the rabble in the slums. He claims they are being mistreated and thinks the government should dole them out free food, as if they are not already bleeding the coffers dry by using the food stamps which are distributed every six months. He also went on protest when dogs were declared illegal in all areas except the slums. Procedure A 89!

5. Kurbus Prule. 59 years old. A bad man. Immoral terrorist and vegetarian crapshooter (? - SHUDENSHEIZER). A former expert on robotomics and computers until he became deranged. He has made fantastic assertions that the "Kumflams" that the government has put in all new houses, cars and televisions – in pursuit of Order 44 Subrule 879 – are spy computers which cause an invasion of privacy. Furthermore he has alarmed the public by claiming these "Kumflams" are linked up to a Daddy Spy Computer (? - DODDLEWUFFKUMFLAM) in the control of the army. These claims have no basis and any member of the public found to believe these should be arrested and charged with Offence K-Special. Procedure ZT 84777!

6. Rakwitt Schlitt. 42 years old. Dangerous. Arrested as a student for having no identity card and a false moustache (? - SLEIMER SLUPPWEIZER). Refuses to cooperate with the military police. Subsequently served two years in the security wing at Dansk. Suspected of writing under an assumed name in foreign journals. Inspectors making any arrest may presume he is armed and dangerous and in disguise. Procedure Ypp 1!

7. Gupzer Hatte. 60 years old. An economics correspondent before he was rightly sacked after making assertions that prominent politicians were pocketing huge amounts from the football coupons and state lottery treasury. A rabble rouser. This man should not be allowed air his

subversive views in pursuit of Order FZ 486. His private mail should be monitored under the Emergency Statute. His telephone should be closely examined (? - EXHORBITED). All contacts should be traced on the security computer. It is suspected that he may have contacts with black gorillas in Africa and illegal strikers in America. Procedure ZT 84777!

8. Lucer Irvork. A dark horse. Very little is known about this terrorist. He is forty-seven years old and can be identified by a pear-shaped mole on the left upper corner of his back. He fronts as a respectable businessman, a hoover salesman, and lives at 40 Greenbogger Gardens. It is at this address that the other seven men listed above attend every Friday under the disguise of playing bridge. These conspirational (? -GABBATWACKER) meetings have been taking place since the 4th January last. This man is particularly dangerous because of his clean computer record, and a menace to our stable democracy. It is also suspected that he has connections with several terrorist groups who are presently in confinement at the Baulox Mental Asylum, but so far he has not slipped up by visiting the hospital in person. Procedure A.89.

And that's them – an ordinary enough sort of bunch who like myself don't get on too well with the army. Of course, there's a lot more stuff to read about them, and photographs, but it drives me to sleep. The last thought I have before I go to the land of nod is that I must get in touch with them and let them know they're in danger of being liquidised no matter what the lawyers in Jerusalem do.

Twenty-Six

All the men in Q-Sector are grinning on the last day of the month and roaming around with moonstruck eyes. Even Herr Windtail is beaming out of himself like as if he had just invented the chocolate marshmallow. And the others are acting strange as well: Ugidet my workmate has turned off his welding machine and is studying the football coupons. Now and again he breaks out into a marching war tune that he whistles out his nose: Bopp-Bopp, du-dah-du-bopp-bopp. . . Then he stops and marks something down on his forms. He obviously thinks he is going to get a treble-X winner and win ten million Kacks.

Herr Ghoulman, who looks after spare parts, is sniggering and showing off his latest pornographic magazine to Fickling and Purdoppe. The only people doing any work are me and Zinky the robot. And even I stop then when I hear someone croaking out my name in the passageway outside. When I investigate this I find there's a computer hot on my trail. It's out at the door flashing a yellow light and calling for me. Stupid machine goes wandering all around the Works getting in everyone's way – it nearly knocked me down one time.

"What d'ye want?" says I.

"Hatz aerodraks!" it says and hands me over two letters. Then it wheels away with itself, and I know you won't believe this, unless you've bothered to read the chapter title – the letters have come all the way from Ireland and I can see straight away that one of them is from the da. He always steals his envelopes from the Registry of Mortgages; he puts on an act that he's as honest as Matt Talbot, but behind it all he's only a petty criminal. He's always bringing home paper clips and rubber bands and stuff that he never uses. And the paper he writes on gives the letter a bad atmosphere because of the official stamp marked at the top of it. While you're reading it you half expect to come across some dead king of England who is urgently looking for rent.

THE REGISTRY OF MORTGAGES
Archives Division,
Dublin 1.
Ref. . . . . . .

Dear Paddy,

Thank you for your charming if somewhat acerbic letter. I am delighted to hear that you are highly impressed with the people and city of Baulox, even if in your humble opinion the Western section is slightly meretricious. Of course, when in Rome do as the Romans do, is an excellent motto.

Your grandfather whom you enquire after is I am sad to say in a strangely atribilious humour, no doubt brought about by the recent closure of the Dublin pubs. Ever since the barmen came out on strike he has been as belligerent as a stickleback out of water and a constant thorn in my side. Which reminds me! I have a serious complaint to make about your so-called friend Jody McGovern: only the other night I caught him attempting to purloin my bicycle from the garden shed. And not only that! The rascal had the dashed impudence to assert in public in the presence of our good neighbour Mrs Horne that the bicycle belonged to him. Damn cheek! I had a good mind to call the police to iron the matter out. Perhaps you would be so good as to ask him, when you return home on your vacation, to curb his criminal tendencies and at the very least to keep away from my garden shed.

I am delighted that you intend to take an early vacation and enclose herewith one air ticket direct from Baulox to Dublin. It would be best if you depart as soon as you receive this letter. There is no need your offering notice at your job for I shall be getting in touch with Herr Blumm shortly.

Regarding your suggestion of purchasing a new sailing boat, I have written today to Gaelic Fiberdingy Ltd for their catalogue which I expect will be awaiting you when you return.

Love,
Da.

And that's the letter! I feel sorry for the da because he is obviously getting geriatric. I never mentioned a word about taking a holiday. I read the letter again. And then again, but I still can't make head or tail of it – the da must be taking drugs or something to hold back his old age; he can't even remember that I sold the bicycle to Jody. And as for the pubs being shut in Dublin, he must be imagining things. The only thing I can think of is to write straight back to him and try and sort his thinking out. This is no easy task because the wages have arrived into Q-Sector and all hell is breaking loose. The workers are standing around in a circle nattering about the computer slips that come in the wage packets. It seems that Ugidet has got a bigger bonus than Herr Windtail.

"Ester guckhandle vom Herr Zuckermutter!" Fickling suggests.

"Nack nack!" says Windtail.

"Fuff Woger!" (Big money) says Ugidet.

"Aawwm!" says Purdoppe.

"Nack nack," says Windtail and on it goes while I try and rip out a letter to the da.

THE WORKS
BAULOX.

Dear Da,

Thanks for your little note but I can't make sense of it at all. Were you off your nuts when you were writing it? What's all this stuff about me taking holidays and I'm only after arriving here a couple of months? And the story about the bicycle: I found that bike outside the Pro-Cathedral on Marlboro Street and sold it to Jody for fifteen quid. It's not yours! You sound like to me that you've had a geriatric attack. And I don't believe the pubs in Dublin are shut. That's an impossibility. . .

"Vas pupt dur dankensleif, ober dixtost? Ober pupt baruma gungst?" says Ugidet. He has come over to me and wants to know what I'm writing, my life story? Or a letter to my girlfriend?

"Agh blumta tort diffensagt gungst!" says Windtail, breaking his pimply face into a snigger. And then he laughs out loud like a car exhaust-pipe explosion. Why he thinks it's funny that I might be writing to my mother-in-law I don't know.

"Shard!" says I, wishing they'd all go way and do some work. I'm starting to feel like a lucky mascot or something the way they're all ganging around me. And it's only then I remember the second letter and I don't believe it – it's from Hairlips! Imagine him writing to me and he never has more than four words to put together at one time! I rip it open.

> Daffy's Lounge Bar,
> Dublin, and don't ask me
> what bleedin date it is cause I don't know nuthin' about it
> cept it's a black saturday night over here and I'm pissing it
> up all on my lonesome and not having a clue what to do
> cause you won't believe it because Micko Jody Gus and some
> other geezer who came out of the pub with us are all locked
> up and on top of that I got to drink bad beer cause guinness
> has gone on strike why I don't have a clue cause they're
> deprivin us of one of our benefactions. A pain in the hole is
> what it is.
>
> I had a bad bellyful of Jodys sister and weve fallen out of
> the idea of hitching ourselves up and you wont believe it
> cause shes puttin on heirs now wantin to get a better catch
> than me and marry upwards into a big house so I told her to
> go and shag herself and you wont believe it cause shes
> stopped cursen and now shes takin night courses in
> improvements. A pain in the hole is what it is.
>
> Its stupid thats what I think tryin to liberate the
> transport ministers mercedes outside the dail where they rig
> up all the votes while the choafer was off for a piss. Must
> have been out of their box and theyd hardly taken off when
> there was seven or eleven squad cars after them. Course I
> wasnt with them cause Im not that daft. I told them they
> were thick and I wasnt goin with them. It was a pain in the
> hole cause a smaller car would have done us just as good
> cause all we wanted to do was take a drive out in the country.
> I told them they were stupid and there was no convincin

Jody and the others were as bad. Micko said that the minister should be made to go on the bus and now hes in jail so thats all I'll say.

LIPS

P.S. Your old man was sayin something to me this morning to write to you and ask you to come home as soon as you can because he said the political climate wasnt suitin your talents. Dont ask me what he was talking about. Hes actin strange these days lockin up his garden shed when he goes to work and not lettin Jody have his bike back though he cant be needin it if hes goin to stay in jail.

P.S.S. Hope you can read this writin cause I cant cause it must be two years since I wrote my last essay about the man drownin in the boat but that fucker what was it off the topic bloody eegit so my spellin is rusty.

HAIRLIPS.

"Dusteroko harterhodd nasho masho?" (Are ye not coming up to gobble a bit of cabbage?) says Ugidet.

"Nisht!" says I. I hadn't even noticed the dinner hooter blasting off, concentrating so hard on Hairlips' letter. At least with Windtail and his cronies out of the way I'd be able to get on with another letter to the da.

THE WORKS,
BAULOX.

Dear Da,
    Got your letter handed today to me by a talking computer and didn't think much of it when I read it. Sounds like

you're breaking out in old age and cracking up. What's all this about holidays and me after only arriving, and the pubs closing and bicycles? You probably need a holiday yourself so I'm sending you back your air ticket.

So much has happened in the last two monhs that it would take a huge book like greatgranda's bible that he probably stole from the monastery after he decided to quit being a priest, to fit it all into and if I did write it all down I don't think even you would bother reading it. As Scut Fagan says – Leave all the bilge, puff and padding to the politicians.

You'll be glad that I've learnt a tremendous amount of Baulox since I last wrote to you. I spent a couple of weeks at the Serbski Institute for Modermask Baulox and was taught the most colossal heap of absolute wogglewash imaginable. Imagine calling a dog a SCHERTERZAMBIST! Sounds like an acrobat. You just wouldn't believe the number of meaningless words they have for the most ordinary things. Of course I jacked in the course before I finished because the LLL or at least my contact in the LLL who I can't name because she said things are hotting up, warned me that the Institute is also used for brainwashing, dragging names out of you with drugs, and tortures of all kinds. Now Herr Ugidet teaches me – he's the guy that works with me and he's a great teacher because he's full up with dirty words. He'd knock a docker flat with the bad language he has in his head. The best thing about him he's not intellectual and doesn't seem to give a wank what order you put your words in, or whether they're absolute adjectives or the other way around. And he doesn't go in for heavy reading – the football coupons is his limit, not that there's much else to read over here except flesh magazines that Ghoulman brings to the job, and the Baulox Press which is a sort of news bulletin and Our Boys paper for the army. It has a fierce bias against the LLL.

Did I tell you about the LLL in my last letter? They're the Live Love Liberate group that go around hijacking aeroplanes and robbing banks. I'm sort of doing a line with one of the women members who got to know me because she went to school with Blumm's secretary Manda. She tells me Manda was always on the make ever since she was about twelve years old. Maybe that's why she usually wears no knickers in her see-through dress, or bras, or anything like that, but she won't let me go near her at all. Her friend is always trying to drag me to LLL meetings and she gave me a present of The Complete Works of Heinzroot Goofthark the biggest gorilla since Dockscheister or someone. I went to one of these meetings once and never again. There was about twenty people there all dressed up in beards and smoking pipes, all very friendly at first until they all started to spoof out political Baulox at the same time and get at each others throats. As you'd call it yourself, it turned into a metabolicksical galimatias. (It's great to be able to shag some of your own big words back at you.)

One thing I can say for your mate Blumm – he had the guts to ask me over to his house the other night to meet his missus. It's the biggest house I was ever in but his missus is a terrible axehead. She wanted to know all about Ireland starting at Moses and going on to when round towers were all the rage. And she feeds Blumm on dog biscuits and that's probably why he goes around all day with that desperate look on his face. Reminds me of what granda said when I asked him why he spent so much time in the pub on Black Pudding Lane. He told me that the grandma, who's your ma, turned herself ino a domestic horror after she went off sex. I'd say the same thing has happened to Missus Blumm. You should write to Blumm and tell him to stand up for his rights.

And was I telling you about an oddball called Krimp who took me one night to a sex club called Bumballims and got beaten up by the army because I landed one on a prominent politician? Although fair play to him – when they let him out of the barracks five weeks later with a broken arm and his teeth all smashed he asked me would I go again with him to the very same club. He cracked a joke about us not finishing our dance. He has his glue. Then was I telling you about Flarsky, the guy they murdered over here? I haven't heard a word about him since. It's been all shushed up.

The job is going alright and I've found out that we are

making nuclear bombs or at least the Essential Ingredients for nuclear bombs. One of the guys in the LLL was very keen that I should draw maps of the Works and try and smuggle them out the Essential Ingredient. I haven't made up my mind about this. As far as I can make out they probably keep the bombs and their Essential Ingredients in the top security BB-Sector which is surrounded by an alarm system called a Klam Klam. This alarm goes very bad bananas if anyone tries to go near the place and so do the gunmen which I saw for myself one day when they nearly shot down two innocent plasterers and a wheelbarrow who had lost their way.

If you have any ideas for shutting up this Klam Klam let me know for if I could get a bomb or the Essential Ingredient out of BB-Sector I might be able to give it to the LLL who might live up to their name then and do something useful with it. That's all I'll say now, the sausage break is over. Tell Jody and the lads the women and the crack over here are ninety-nine point nine and I'm out on the piss every night of the week. And tell granda I was asking for him.

Love,
Paddy.

The next thing I have to do after I finish the letter is phone up one of the Eight Sane Men and try and give them their life stories back. Missus Echolle wants them out of her house. And it takes me ages to get through to one of them. They are either not at home or won't answer but finally a man's voice comes over:. "Straffel?" he says.

"Is that Lucer Irvork?" says I.

"Speaking," says he.

Twenty-Seven

INVITATION TO PLAY BRIDGE WITH THE EIGHT SANE MEN AT 40 GREENBOGGER GARDENS AND A QUICK DRINK WITH THE MEN FROM WORK.

"Hallo," says I, "I'm just ringing to find out if you want your life histories back from the army?"

"Who is that speaking?"

"Paddy Murphy from Ireland."

"You are phoning from Ireland?" says Irvork.

"No, I'm just down the road. Do you want all those papers?"

"What papers do you speak of?"

"Ye know – all about you and the other seven fellahs that play bridge together. I found them one day when they were beating me up in the army barracks."

"So you are from Ireland and wish to play bridge. . ."

"Bridge?" says I.

"Yes, we will be delighted to fit you into a few rubbers. Come to my house Friday evening next. Do you play the Italian Club System?" he says.

"But I don't know a thing about bridge," says I.

"Oh, so you are a beginner. Never mind, we are not exactly experts ourselves."

"Ober telesplotter pupt derdeke gungst!" says Ugidet.

"Ah piss off!" says I.

"Har hawh hawh!" goes Windtail, breathing pickled cabbage into my face.

"And about the papers?" says I.

"Yes, yes, yes, bring your own playing cards if you wish."

"Listen Windtail, will you go and shag off!" says I. Because they think I'm phoning up my girlfriend they're acting like morons.

"Binga, binga, binga!" says Windtail, pretending to do an imaginary wank with his closed fist, and spluttering into an outrageous laugh. I don't know who's the worst – him or the lunatic on the phone that's crapping on about bridge. The da used to play bridge with three ladies from the Irish Countrywoman's Sodality and it was the most boring thing I ever saw in my life.

"But it's not really what I phoned up about," says I.

"Yes, yes, if you want to buy a hoover we'll discuss it over schnapps!"

"Hoover?"

"Yes, and I must warn you we play for two Kacks a thousand."

"I'd say they're going to liquidise youz if you don't watch out. . ."

"I do not speak English so very good so we will see you next Friday night. Goodbye!" says Irvork and puts down his phone. The bloody eejit doesn't seem to give a damn what the army is going to do to him. Bridge is all he cares about.

"Ah shut up!" says I to Windtail and the others as I try and go back to work. It's some job! All afternoon Q-Sector remains in a tizzy of excitement − it's as if the moon had turned green. And as soon as the last hooter of the day blasts off the whole seven of us are out the door like a shot and on our way to a bar at the top of the Gump called the Hugger-schnortz Taverna. It's the Baulox tradition to have a few drinks with the men on payday so the pub is jam packed and spilling out into the street. And it's not only the men from the Works are there − the whole factory population of the Gump seem to be on the piss. You wouldn't believe the noise!

After a lot of manoeuvering and shoving the seven of us somehow manage to commandeer a little space at the bar and get down to some serious drinking. And then all sorts of transformations and mutations take place; Windtail who is normally the sourest prune in the bag turns into a laughing cavalier. Purdoppe who is usually as morose as a cow in three feet of snow starts spouting out of him like a comedian. A wicked gleam spreads itself over Duaditty's face and by Jazus! What a thundering uproar! The others, Ghoulman, Fickling and my mate Ugidet start singing.

DAST FUMPTER STOONK
HAR DAR BARMFART KUFT
DEE DONK HORR HORR
MORR MORR MORR MORR

and they keep on repeating this verse, and clapping their hands, banging their feet and slapping me on the back. You'd think we were after winning a world war.

Later when it fades out a bit Ugidet and me get into a conversation about welding.

"Si kumpt dastrip gutzleken erloafin juuust!" he says, comparing his penis to the welding rod. It would be a disgrace to translate it exactly.

"Bopo muxtapp," says I. (I suppose so.)

"Dunkoffe ghullbeit shard nik curney stalt! Ha! Ha!" he says and then makes an outrageous suggestion to explain this. He has a very earthy mind.

"Oh fucking hell!" says I getting up and pretending to go to the jax. The crack is ninety but with the noise and the sweat and Ugidet's dirty jokes I have to get out of there. As I'm heading across the carpark who do I see only Blumm's secretary Manda and Zuckermutter flirting together in her yellow sportscar. I go over to them friendly as can be and give a rap on the window. Manda is sitting behind the wheel and she buzzes down the window. For some reason neither of them seem too glad to see me.

"How is the crack?" says I.

"Have you information to import to me?" says Zuckermutter.

"You should go into the pub," says I, "it's a riot. Windtail is actually singing in there."

"If you have information to import you must be in attendance in my office following me on a Wednesday," says Zuckermutter.

"What?" says I.

"We are at conference with personal business," he says.

"Ah, get up the yard. I know what you're up to," says I.

"Thank you, Herr Murphy, that will be all," says Manda buzzing up her window again. It's the first snub I ever got in my life and it drives me over to the bus stop in a lousy bad humour.

And the humour improves worse because only minutes later when Manda pulls in beside me in the bus stop and offers me a lift, I'm so pissed off that I tell her to get lost. And then I'm kicking myself as I watch her car turn itself into a small yellow dot on the Highway, because the da had told me often enough never to refuse a reasonable offer, and if I do, to be polite about it. By the time the bus gets to picking me up I'm almost coming around to thinking that he might be right in some ways.

Twenty-Eight

THE ESSENCE OF A BAD HUMOUR. A LAST MINUTE TRIBUTE TO HERR FLARSKY, AND WHISKERSLOOSH AT PEDRA'S BAR.

A rotten humour that gets a person's goat up is a contrarious obstacle to an enjoyable life. On the bus back to City Centre I'm still brooding over Herr Zuckermutter and Manda — I'd like to kill the bastard, or at least punch him one on the nose. It's easy to see what drives a person to murder — bad manners.

When I get out at the bus depot the neon lights in the West Sector attract me like a wasp to the jam factory, and I wander in the general direction of Pedra's bar. It's hard to get the picture of Zuckermutter out of my head, him and Manda giving me the brush as if they had something important to talk about. Bloody snobs wouldn't even go in to hear Windtail roaring his head off. I can think of several things I should have said to them and didn't.

It's hard to know what's got into me, for without thinking I stick my letter to the da into a post box up near Scuntza Taverna, and it's only after it has dropped that I want it back. It suddenly dawns on me that I should have taken the air ticket and the next plane to Dublin, so I'm standing there like an eejit sticking my arm into the slit. It's no use, I can't reach the letter, and I honestly think if I had a sledgehammer I would knock the post box to smithereens. In fact I look around to see if there is anything heavy to hand but there's nothing. I know it's crazy and I can see the headlines: IRISHMAN GOES BERSERK IN BAULOX AND ATTACKS POST BOX, so I forget about it, and go on up the street. There are a few redneck bouncers and whores hanging out at the dooway of Scuntza Taverna and I'm thinking of crossing over to the other side of the street to avoid them until I remember Flarsky and the two thugs who wouldn't catch his joke at the bar. I head straight towards them.

I'm not a guy that ever looks for trouble but all the same I think it's right to go in and see if the two thugs are there. Flarsky risked his life for me that night and lost, so it's only proper to set things right. I have to pay out a few Kacks to get in but I don't mind that — you can't put a price on anger. The bouncers make me sign a visitors' book and one of the whores asks me would I like some SNUUZEY. I ignore her and go on in.

It's just as I remembered, like the insides of a spaceship gone wrong with a lot of people squirming about in the shadows. I go straight over to the curved bar and order a double shagg, and when it comes I pick it up and turn to a couple of gougers who are standing beside me and repeat Flarsky's last joke as loud as I can: "Dab suck Fluchers marstafft, ach sie jaxdunkt flurt donk!" says I. There follows an astonished silence and this time I'm ready for them: if one of them so much as comes near me, I'll flatten him. Cowardly bastards, they sort of edge slowly away from me. They'll attack you from behind but they're afraid to go near you when you are waiting and ready. The woman with the bubbling boobs who is sitting with her legs crossed like she was looking for a part in an ancient French film moves to another seat. Her face is painted up like a Chinese mask and she's wearing a skirt that's too small for her. Everyone seems to be afraid of me for some reason.

"Dab suck Fluchers marstafft, ach sie jaxdunkt flurt donk!" says I again. The gougers move further back. I count to ten: one, two, three, four, five, six, seven, eight, nine, ten, and not one of them squares up to me. I put down my drink and walk straight out. It isn't much but I guess it's some sort of tribute to the dead comedian.

Back on the street my humour for some reason changes for the better and I even find myself laughing at Flarsky's joke and forgetting all about Zuckermutter. I go around to Pedra's and find the pub is crowded with revolutionaries and Zi is sitting on her own at the bar reading a book.

"How'ye!" says I. "What's the book?"

"Oh Paddy! I was just thinking about you."

"Were you? What are you reading?"

"The diaries of Tarid Mann."

"Never heard of him. What'll you have?"

"No thank you, I don't want a drink. You must have heard of Tarid Mann! Have you not finished Heinzroot Goofthark's work yet? He mentioned Tarid Mann several times."

"No. I haven't quite finished it," says I. (I haven't gone past the first page – the book is like one of the stories Shakespeare wrote for the schools, written backwards with a heap of arithmetic and geography books thrown in for confusion, but I don't like Zi to think I don't appreciate her gift.)

"Sure you won't have a drink?"

"Okay if you must, you can get me a sour whisky."

"Right you be. Zarten tuppa bly whiskersloosh apt shagg!" says I to the barman. Zi sticks her nose right back into the book.

"What did he do anyway?" says I.

"Who?"

"This guy you're reading."

"Oh. Tarid Mann was a famous urban gorilla."

"Was he the fellah in China that went on the huge walk?"

"Paddy, I'm surprised at you. Anyone with the slightest education has heard of Tarid Mann!"

"Not me. Scut Fagan or the Christian Brothers never mentioned him."

"Paddy, the Christian Brothers are of no consequence."

"I wouldn't say that, that's where me and Jody and the lads got all our learning."

"Which is not a great deal if you don't know about Heinzroot and Tarid Mann."

"They're foreigners! I bet you, you don't know about Micko, the greatest revolutionary since the sliced pan, and he doesn't need a beard to do it!"

"Micko?"

"Yea, or Raftery the Snake that can make a bomb out of a box of matches, or Dick Muldoon or any of those?"

"No, I must admit they don't sound familiar."

"Then there you are, there's no need to be getting at me about Goofhork or Beetroot!"

"Paddy, please! Have some respect!"

"Zarten tuppa bly whiskersloosh apt shagg!" says I to the barman. We argue on then about more foreigners she knows, and I know you won't believe this but the drink goes straight to my head. After a few more glasses of the stuff I make a terrible slip of the tongue and tell her that I'll smuggle the Essential Ingredient for a nuclear bomb out of the Works and give it over to the LLL.

"No bother," says I, "I'll just slip it out one afternoon when nobody is watching."

"You will!" she says.

"Sure." But then I'm hoping she won't take me serious but she does.

"You promise?"

"I'll see what I can do," says I.

"Oh Paddy! That's the best news I've heard all week!" I'm pleased to see how happy she is — as if I'd promised her a box of Arabian chocolates. Then she tells me I must immediately fix up an appointment with the hierarchy of the LLL.

"But I don't want to meet anyone."

"You must, we have little time, and every hour lost is another one of us in prison. Come on, we'll leave now. We can't phone from here."

"I want to have another drink."

"Okay Paddy, but just one!"

"Zarten tuppa bly whiskersloosh apt shagg!" says I, wondering what I'm getting myself into.

Twenty-Nine

Secret meeting with Kamam, the founder member (dokenspielenkregg dastard) and leader (daf turbak) of the LLL (Lisvervookt Lamelhorne Latvanegtrippensplott) and trained under Dookmeister, the greatest urban gorilla since Julius Caesar.

The hierarchy of the LLL is a mysterious thing and it takes extraordinary amounts of precautions before we can meet anyone. We spend hours in Zi's little blue car driving around in circles from one telephone box to another.

"Why can't we just go straight to whoever we want to see?" says I.

"Paddy, we must take precautions."

"Oh Jazus." It's as hard as trying to find the man who steals your taxes, and I know because I went after him one day when I was working in the beetroot factory in Bristol. Later we have to change cars – don't ask me why. Then Zi has to learn off some passwords and finally we meet up with two gorillas who take me off in an ice cream van. It's mad! They make me wear a hood over my head when we're driving into the heart of the slums and won't let Zi come with us – she goes back to Pedra's bar to wait for me. I don't like it and feel like a pig being led to the slaughterhouse.

It grows into a nightmare, I'm dragged out of the van, manhandled this way and that, shoved in and out of an elevator, and generally abused. Naturally I do a lot of complaining, kicking and trying to get the hood off my head, but it's no use. The gorillas aren't human. Then they push me into a room and I hear them locking the door. And I'm about to scream until I hear someone speaking. I thought I had been locked into a coalhouse or something.

"So this is the wild Irishman!" says somebody.

"Take this thing off my head!"

"Patience, patience. . ." and only then do they unzip the hood, and I find myself face to face with Kamam, the founder member and leader of the LLL who was trained under Dookmeister and was supposed to be a living legend. Zi had told me all about him, and even showed me a scrapbook with all his photographs – the most wanted man in Baulox.

"Will you have a cigar?" is the first thing he says to me, offering me a big fat cigar almost as big as a truncheon.

"I don't smoke," says I.

"What a shame! And these are the best available. . ." And doesn't he go on for about five minutes talking about his blasted cigars. I don't listen too much because it's obvious the guy is an escaped lunatic of some sort. There is a mad glare beaming out his eyes that would stop a clock.

"Let us stop beating about the bush!" he says suddenly.

"How d'ye mean?"

"You have volunteered to assist us, how do you say, remove Daf Einfanb!"

"The what?"

"The Essential Ingredient!"

"Oh yea, the thing for the bomb."

"Exactly. And what method do you propose for securing this Einfanb?"

"Well, I haven't worked it out yet."

"Do not worry, we may very well have a plan. All you will have to do is follow orders passed to you by our agent in the Works."

"D'ye have an agent in the Works?"

"We have several but for the moment you must need only concern yourself with one. Do you happen to know a Manda Zerinisky?"

"What! Blumm's secretary!"

"Yes, I see you know her. One of our most trusted members. Of course, when we set up a provisional government she will be rewarded with a responsible post."

"And are you going into government?" says I.

"I should certainly expect so!" says Kamam nearly knocking me down with his mad glare. The man is off his rocker with his imaginary government and from what I can gather he'd probably give himself a well paid job in it as well – become a minister or some sort of prominent politician. But the amazing thing is hearing that Manda is in the LLL.

"It's hard to believe that she's in your group," says I.

"Yes. An excellent agent! She has given us more inside information than any other two agents of ours about the Works."

"I must tell Blumm!" says I. Bloody bitch spying on him all the time, and right on top of all that he built. I know he never had two Kacks to rub together when he was my age, and then building up his monstrous empire singlehanded only to be waited on by traitors and a hawk-faced wife. You'd have to feel sorry for him.

"You must tell who?" says Kamam.

"Only joking," says I and he laughs.

"We know more about you, Mister Murphy, than you might think; we have heard about your exploits with the army – we know what side you are on!"

"Yea?" Again I have to look away from his eyes. On the wall behind him is a huge black and red poster showing a hairy-faced lunatic with a sten gun. There is a big bubble of words coming out his mouth – FAKTER MASTRIGG ORGANIZATIONALES INTERNAZIONALIST TROPT!

"Who's your man?" says I.

"Dookmeister – my former commander."

"Oh yea, I heard about him, used to be a revolutionary or something."

"He still is."

"I thought Zi said he'd been shot."

"His spirit lives on," says Kamam, waving his big cigar around in a circle. It's getting very hard to breathe. And I'm wondering why he wears short trousers with green and pink splodges on them, but I don't say anything. They warned me at home to be slow to remark on a person's dress when it's a bit peculiar. He has bumpy little fat legs and big boots.

"Like the catholics!" says I.

"How do you mean?"

"Their spirits live on too, even if they get shot in the head."

"No, no, Dookmeister! Never! I do not understand your logic." Another peculiar thing about him is the pair of binoculars hanging from his neck and there isn't a window in the place. It's like he's dressed up for a British war film but I don't say anything.

"A dangerous looking character," says I.

"Yes, a dangerous man to cross I must admit."

"I'd say that," says I looking over at the two gorillas who are still standing at the door. They haven't opened their mouths since I've seen them. I wonder why they don't sit down or even stand somewhere else.

"And now if we may return to the business at hand," says Kamam.

"There's nothing much more to say," says I, wanting to get the hell out of there and go for a drink. I have to look everywhere except into his eyes. He has a sort of a square face with a round head on it that's as bald as a peeled onion.

"Yes, perhaps you are right. You will receive further instructions from Miss Zerinisky, and of course you will not breathe a word of this meeting to anyone."

"No, I won't say a word."

"Well, it has been a pleasure meeting you."

"Thanks," says I and at a signal from Kamam the two gorillas start putting the hood over my head, but it's all a waste of time because while they're fixing it on I see Kamam's address printed squarely across an electricity bill on the table at the door: 50B Flapp Street. And it's the last thing I see before everything turns black. Before we head off Kamam says one more thing to me. "And remember," he says, "we will have a need of business connections in Ireland in the near future."

"What?" I try and speak through the hood but I can't hear my own words.

"Yes, we may very well find a position for you," says Kamam and his two gorillas lead me away.

Thirty

I LOSE MY VIRGINITY, OR AT LEAST I THINK I DO.

It's just as complicatory getting back from Kamam's as it was getting there. More passwords and a long ride in the back of an ice cream van leaves me back in Pedra's bar talking to Zi.

"That Kamam fellah is. . ."

"Shhhish!" says Zi interrupting me in mid-sentence. I was about to tell her he was a lunatic.

"What's up?" says I.

"We can't speak here."

"Well, let's go to The Harbour Bar," says I.

"Okay, Paddy."

"All I was going to say was. . ."

"Shhhish!" she says again. It's an annoying habit she has. Obviously she doesn't want to hear anything about Kamam, but when we get out to her car she's all questions. How tall is he? Does he carry a gun? What sort of voice does he speak with?

"You mean you never met him?"

"Only at a distance."

"Well, he's like an American actor with a Russian accent playing a part in a British war film who has just escaped out of a lunatic asylum in a pair of boy scout's trousers."

"Paddy, you must not speak with disrespect about Kamam our leader!"

"Why? What did he ever do for me?"

"Kamam is the most important man in Baulox!"

"He wears the most important pair of pants maybe."

"What brand does he wear?" she says and after I explain to her about the pants we get to talking about me growing up in Dublin. And Jody and the lads. And by this time we're sitting in The Harbour Bar in the corner with the drunks. As usual they're out of their skulls and grinning at me for they seem to like me ever since I came into the bar all covered in blood. Now and then they crack funny remarks at us and Herr Echolle, who doesn't want to hear anything because he's trying to concentrate on a railway that he's building at the back of the bar.

"But Dublin is nothing like Baulox!" says I.

"Paddy, all FFF cities are the same!"

"No, Dublin is different."

"Why is it?"

"Because we don't speak Baulox, and Jody and the lads live over there, and the granda and the da."

"You will have to grow up and break your old ties."

"And it's more than that. There's a different atmosphere, all the clocks over there tell different times, and you can shout on the streets without the Baulox Army beating your head in."

"Paddy, you are still a child at heart."

"And what about yourself?"

"It is not very interesting."

"Why did you come over to Baulox?"

"I was born here."

"Here!" says I. It's hard to imagine anyone being born in Baulox. It turns out she's the only daughter of a man who owns a big building with slot machines in it. He has lots of money because people keep coming back to lose their money in his machines. These people must be daft.

"That is why I left home, because he is a capitalist!"

"But you can't blame him if people want to put all their money in his machines."

"I'm not blaming my father, I am blaming the system!"

"Oh?"

"That is also why I went to Belfast in your country."

"Why?"

"To learn how to defeat the system."

"You would have done better to come to Dublin," says I and then she lets it out that she was kicked out of school like myself.

"That's gas! They threw me out too for beating up my English teacher. Why did they kick you out?"

"Because of my politics."

"I thought they loved politics in school."

"No, our policy was that all education must stop! Now!" she says raising up her voice like as if I was a half a mile away.

"Oh!" says I.

What happened was, she had incited a riot or something at the Kramatorium High School and a certain Missus Shipeschooner had taken the matter up from there. I gather she was a very bad bitch. And also Trotsky and somebody else from the bible had something to do with it.

But she tells me I can't understand because I haven't enough political awareness.

"What has politics got to do with the price of onions?" says I.

"It is something a man has or hasn't."

"Yea?" says I and she breaks into a story about a man called Karl who she had lived with at Art School but he had turned over to The Authority and that was unforgivable.

"Turned what over?" says I.

"He changed his whole way of painting."

"That doesn't sound too bad."

"Yes, but he started painting the way The Authority told him."

"And you didn't like that?" says I.

"Let us not talk about him any more. What about us? What we must do now is go to your room and make love."

"Okay," says I. It sounds like a good idea to me especially because I never did it before. I'd often thought about it but it's always better to put the idea into practice, and it shouldn't be any bother for I'd seen thousands at it on the films. And then she leans over and kisses me on the mouth. Jazus! I thought the drunks were asleep but they wake up and start clapping and laughing.

"Paddy, you must be the slowest man I've ever gone out with."

"I nearly broke the four minutes once," says I.

"I mean to say, we have been to all those horrible movies and not once have you thought to kiss me."

"I must have forgot," says I.

"Then show me up to your room before you forget again," she says and I bring her upstairs to the thunderous applause of the drunks. They sound like they're really enjoying themselves. I find that she's not very slow herself − we're hardly in the door and she has ripped off half our clothes. Next she is lying starkers on the bed and I'm making a flying jump at her. The shoving and poking starts and soon we're bouncing up and down as if we're on a trampoline. She scrawbs at me like a mad cat and I keep on poking but I can't get the blasted thing in. Then she goes over on top of me, and the next thing is we're in the air with her arse to the ceiling − I ram it home and we start going like the clappers of BeJazus.

"Tell me," says I as the lampshade starts swinging like a pendulum.

"OOOOH!" she says.

"Why didn't you tell me Manda was in the LLL?" The springs are starting to screech out of them like a train crash.

"OOH! So you know. I wasn't allowed tell you."

"And who are the other agents there?" says I as we're slapping all over the room. She starts biting my ear and on we go like a crazy yo-yo for a couple of hours. Great fun, but I don't remember much more about it except waking up as if in a dream to hear Missus Echolle knocking on the door. She opens it and sticks her head in.

"Oh, you have found a friend at last."

"Yea," says I, wondering if I'd lost my virginity and thinking I must have because the room looks like a tornado had come in the window.

"Perhaps now you give up the drink. For a young man you drink too much!"

"You must be joking! Sure Zi here had me drunk under the table."

"Good morning, are you a friend of Paddy's?" she says as Zi begins to come to. She seems very puzzled by the surroundings.

"Who are you?" says Zi.

"I am the proprietress." It's funny but the two women don't seem to get on too well together and I'm sort of glad when Missus Echolle goes off.

"I don't think I'll bother to go to work," says I to Zi.

"But, Paddy, you must, you have to make arrangements about Daf Einfanb."

"The what?"

"The Essential Ingredient."

"Oh hell!" says I. I had forgotten all about the bloody bomb.

"Paddy, take a few of these," says Zi offering me some pills.

"No, I don't take medicine."

"They are only Energy Tablets – Lef Hoktarts. You'll feel better after taking a couple."

"Oh alright, give us them," says I and swallow down four or five of them. A bit of glucose won't do me any harm. And later as I'm going out she calls me back.

"And Paddy!"

"What?" She's still sitting on the edge of the bed with a sort of a lost look in her eyes. She's beautiful.

"Be careful!"

"Sure," says I, and I go off to catch the bus to work. I'm wondering will she be there when I come back.

Thirty-One

It's strange, I don't know whether it's all the whiskersloosh and shagg, or because I've given away my virginity, or because of the tablets, but by the time I get to the bus I'm feeling like a different person — I don't feel like Paddy Murphy at all. I'm tensed up and all I can think of is liberating the Essential Ingredient, Daf Einfanb, and my stomach is tight like a knot. I've decided that I'm going to try and get Daf Einfanb singlehanded; for some reason I'm not very much in love with Kamam, the leader of the LLL. In the back of my mind I'm thinking the Eight Sane Men might be better people to give the bomb to, and I've to see them in a couple of days time for a game of bridge. I'd have to act quick.

One problem is that the whole of Baulox has taken on a different look than it had before. Maybe it's the light? A pale patch of sunlight edges its way through the grey sky and it makes the people on the bus look very tired and resigned. It's like they know they have been travelling for a long long time to somewhere they don't want to go, but they also know there is no way back. It's weird and like what the da calls Deja Vu — I think I've seen a film of it before, a ghost story of some kind.

Off we go in the bus, purring along the yellow line in the centre of the Highway. It's like everything has been taken out of our control and we've no choice about where we're going yet nobody seems to care. The man beside me in the grey suit only pretends to be reading the *Baulox Press*. Then he looks at his watch although he knows what time it is, and back to the paper, and I look away out the window. We seem to be going in slow motion and I'm seeing a lot of things I hadn't noticed before.

The Baulox Highway is a bit like a long prick with a hard on it: it hammers away all day at the Gump at the top, and goes flabby again in the evening. A high black wall runs straight up along the West side of the highway and this is cluttered up with women in bikinis advertising beer, sausages, Coko and Danko Oil and smiling out with big white teeth. Behind the wall is the Goosshitch Area where there used to be a lot of nuclear electricity stations, but Ugidet my workmate told me they all melted away one night and now there is nothing in there. This is hard to

109

believe although it's impossible to see what's behind the wall because of the big cloud of grey gas that hangs over the place.

At periods along the wall there are small concrete boxes. I had often wondered what they were for but now I can see there are gunmen in them. What they are guarding I don't know. At the top of the Highway the wall curves away and around the Gump where all the factories are. Narrow roads leak like veins from the Highway to various parts of the Gump.

I get off at the second road and walk a hundred yards to the entrance to the Works. This is a small gate in the thirty foot high metal fence. A gunman stands on either side. Usually there is a queue here but not this morning because I'm late. The procedure is simple enough. The left gunman checks the number disc on my jacket with the numbers on a pink sheet of paper while the right gunman threatens to shoot me. They wave me on to the next barbed wire fence at the carpark. Same procedure. I pass on into the Kruzgoff, the metal security chute, past the X-ray machine and into the Search Office. There I am put against the wall, and hand searched. Routine. From there I walk down a narrow passageway where all the safety regulations (Daf Dukswallopo) are plastered on the walls, and out the open door. At this point I am in the Works proper and can go anywhere I want.

There are about four different routes I can take. Usually I go to the right down past the aluminium tower with the circular dome on top, through the toolroom door and down the stairs to Q-Sector, but as I want to take another look at BB-Sector where I think the Essential Ingredient is stored, I take the left turn into the Administration Block. There I suddenly remember that Zuckermutter has shortchanged me in the wages, and by opening his door without knocking I catch him reading *Bumkoffer*, which is a heavy porn magazine.

"Gusto Morg, Herr Murphy, I notice you do not knock at my door to show your courtesy," he says putting the magazine into a steel filing cabinet. I could almost speak better Baulox than he can English but I leave it be.

"You still owe me some money from my first month's wages," says I.

"Herr Murphy, I have an explanation offered before that your appointment at the beginning was to work as a Schimmelblugger and not as an operator in welding."

"But I never worked as a Blugger – Windtail does all that. You can

110

ask Ugidet or any of the others: all I ever did in Q-Sector was weld, so you owe me thirty-eight Kacks.''

''Herr Murphy, this affair with me is growing tired so I will undertake to have the matter examined at the end of the month.''

''But this is only the first day of the month and I should have got that money ages ago. You can hardly expect a man to wait three months for his wages.''

''Herr Murphy, is it that you have forgot who exactly you are talking to? I am Herr Zuckermutter! Director of Everything Personal! There are numerous fields of responsibility which I must examine. The matter with wages is only part.''

''All I want are my wages.''

''Herr Murphy! I will undertake to have the matter thrown into the light. Suffice?''

''Yea okay, good luck.''

''Bumbowl,'' he says and I go on down the corridor and across an open square to BB-Sector.

It had all seemed so simple in the pub and when I was talking to Kamam. All I'd have to do would be wait for the gunmen to go off for their sausages and Coko, turn off the Klam Klam alarm, walk into BB-Sector, take the Essential Ingredient and hide it somewhere in the Works until I figured a way to get it out. And Bob's your uncle!

But the reality is a bit different. For starters only three of the gunmen go off for Coko and sausages. The other three stay in the glass office at the edge of the BB perimeter which is the red line surrounding the building. All along this line there are warnings – DIEKUNG! NUK STROFFTER! PERZONALES NAKT VEGEN VITEST STROFFTER!

I don't really know what to do and I'm standing there for quite a while, and then I think that surely they won't mind me having a look into the BB warehouse. Pretending all innocence I walk across the line in the direction of the open door. Jesus wept! The Klam Klam alarm goes off, sounding like a new religion gone daft, and it's difficult to pretend I don't hear it. I walk on towards the door. And then time seems to slow up a lot and the distance between me and the door stretches. I go on and I'm just at the doorway and get a glimpse of the Essential Ingredient when the bullets hit me in the back.

I don't feel sore or anything, it's like a few mosquitos had attacked me, but I realise that something has gone badly wrong, and I'm thinking of how silly a lot of things are, and the next thing I know is I'm flat out on a hospital bed.

Part Three

Daf Wuirst!
(The End)

Thirty-Two

It must be like waking out of the grave, and the first person I see is the da standing beside my bed. He has a pipe in his mouth and a giant box of matches in his hands, and he looks horribly serious. As usual he can't light the pipe properly because the black stuff Flannigan of Ringsend sells him is not burnable – he may as well put a lump of wet turf in his pipe and puff away at that.

"Why the Jazus don't you get some ordinary tobacco?" says I, but my voice only comes out in a strained whisper, and suddenly I'm wondering where I am and what's going on. I don't recognise anything in the room.

"What did you say, Paddy?" he says.

"I can't talk right," says I, and again I can't even hear myself. The da strikes another match, takes a puff, and his pipe goes out again. He doesn't seem to notice.

"How are you feeling now, Paddy?" he says but I can't answer. I'm trying to figure out what's going on and my eyes keep closing on me.

"I expect you are in some pain," says the da.

"Awwe!" says I.

"So I will leave you to rest a while," he says, and I nearly lose him then because he's halfway out the door before I drag up the energy to shout after him.

"Hey da!" He stands there hesitating like he wants me to sleep or something. It's a bit of a fright the way he's carrying on, not explaining to me what's happening.

"Hey!"

He slowly comes back then to the bed and I'm sure it's only a nightmare of some sort. There's a terrible pain in my side. It seems like I'm swimming in a tank of gas.

"I think you should rest, Paddy," he says.

"Where am I?"

"You are in the Baulox General Hospital."

"Oh Christ!" says I. I thought I was in Dublin and it's only then I remember about walking into the BB-Sector.

"You were taken in three weeks ago," says the da.

"No," says I. It doesn't make sense. I wonder is the da playing tricks on me. Maybe I'm in a mental asylum or somewhere – he always thought I wasn't the full penny.

"Perhaps you cannot remember?" he says.

"Oh God!" says I. The pain is in my chest now.

"What's the matter, Paddy?"

"I want to go home," I whisper.

"All in good time – Doctor Grubbels tells me you are responding well to his treatment."

"Doctor who?"

"Doctor Grubbels."

"Never heard of him."

"You have been unconscious for some time."

"How long?"

"Quite a while – until the day before yesterday."

"You mean I was here yesterday?"

"Yes indeed, you were talking to me yesterday."

"I was not!"

"Now Paddy, I must allow you rest. It's quite late at night as it is."

"I want to go home."

"Now Paddy, Doctor Grubbels has told me you have to stay put for a fortnight."

"Oh God! Are you sure this isn't a mental hospital?" says I, and the da breaks out into a laugh. He always had a curious sense of humour.

"What's funny about that? Here I am on my last legs and you're breaking your hole laughing at me," says I, and I must close my eyes or something, for when I look up again the da has gone and I'm all alone in a small cell-like room. Perhaps I was imagining things? There is a bottle of orange juice and a glass on the bedside locker but nothing much else in the room. Through the small window to my right with the metal grid I can see it's starting to get dark. It's peculiar quiet and then I remember something which makes me scared: the LLL had warned me about the Baulox General Hospital. It wasn't quite what it seemed.

Lots of LLL members had gone into the Baulox Hospital and had somehow come out with different personalities. They go in as bright-eyed revolutionaries and come out like Herr Zuckermutter or somebody like that. I'm not quite sure of the details but it didn't sound good. It seems the army has a big influence in the hospital and they use it like the Serbski Institute for Modermask Baulox for conducting weird experiments. I feel an urgent need to get out of there as quick as I can, but

116

even so my body wants to lie in the bed a bit longer, just like those mornings the da would be trying to get me up for school, only worse.

It takes a lot of agony to raise myself up and slide onto the floor and I'm immediately dizzy. Imagine! And I can't even walk two yards without wobbling and falling on my ear.

"Oh Christ!" says I. I crawl over to the bedside locker and open it, and inside there's nothing except some sort of plastic flower vase. Naturally I'm wondering where my clothes are. I get myself up again and stumble along the wall to the door − it's locked. I try the window but it won't open. I sit down on the edge of the bed, sweat pouring out of me. They have me locked up like a common prisoner and I don't like the idea.

All sorts of ideas come crowding into my head. Maybe I should tie up a load of sheets? Or hide behind the door with the bottle of orange and knock out whoever came in with the breakfast? Stupid ideas generally. And then I notice the small service hatch on the wall opposite me. It too is locked but it's only made of thin plywood − I wrap up the bottle of orange juice in a sheet and smash it to pieces. There's no going back now even if someone heard me: I reach in and find the bolt that's holding it and slide it back.

Out I go head first and land in a heap on the tiled floor of a short corridor. There is a closed door at either end. Through one I hear people moaning so of course I avoid that and take the other door into a brightly lit passageway where the sight of two men in white coats at a desk makes me duck into the first room I come to. Oh Jazus! When I flip on the light I'm very sorry I ever went in − there are corpses in there and bits of them cut off and put in white plastic containers with vinegar or something.

I'm going to get sick because I've never seen a corpse before. And I'm shivering cold so I grab the white coat off the hook, and I'm putting this on when one of the corpses lets out a terrible fart. That puts the panic into me and I run over to the window, open it, and leap out, not much caring how many flights up it was, and I can see the da reading the newspaper headlines − PADDY MURPHY JUMPS OUT WINDOW OF BAULOX HOSPITAL AND BREAKS HIS NECK. But as luck has it I land safely on my ear about six feet below on a flat roof. It's fairly easy going after that; I limp across the roof, down an old metal stairway into the hospital grounds, over the railings onto the street, and straight home to The Harbour Bar keeping to the shadows so that people won't notice I'm only wearing pyjamas and a white coat. I get some queer looks, but they probably figure out I'm going to a fancy dress party in one of the niteclubs.

Thirty-Three

I make a sort of dramatic entry into The Harbour Bar. The place hasn't changed much since I was in last – Mister Echolle is still working on his railway set at the bar, and the drunks are in their usual corner as blotto as ever. They seem to take a curious delight in seeing me. "Bravo!" one of them says, and the others adopt big grins on their faces. Of course I see in the mirror that they're laughing at my appearance – I'm barefoot, in a pair of golden yellow pyjamas and a white coat that is splotched with red dye. I've never seen anything before that disturbed Mister Echolle's interest in his toy trains but he gets up immediately and pulls down the shutters on the window. Then he dims down the light.

"Where have you been?" he asks me.

"I was shot!" says I.

"So that explains it," he says.

"Yea, I'd better go up and change."

"Two men came," he says mysteriously.

"Yea?"

"Clumsy oafs!" he mutters under his breath.

"Pardon?"

"You had better go up to your room and I will call my wife."

"Okay," says I, and I go on upstairs where I find my room is in bits. The mattress has been torn asunder, and my clothes and things are all over the floor. It was in a mess when I left it, but not that bad. Then Missus Echolle comes running in on top of me. She seems very excited.

"There have been two men here in your absence!" she says.

"Yea, I heard."

"I told them I knew nothing!" she says and goes on talking at eleven to the half-dozen. At first I can't understand what she's on about but the picture gradually comes out. What happened was, on the day they shot me down from behind two big surly men had arrived into The Harbour Bar with very important looking documents which they said gave them the right to search the premises. When they didn't find anything they wanted to take away with them, they started wrecking the place, and in doing so they smashed one of Mister Echolle's favourite trains, the one

119

that went to the Orient. Later they questioned everyone in the bar about certain papers they said they were looking for, and terrorised some of the drunks downstairs. It occurs to me that these papers might be the ones I'd stolen off the army about the Eight Sane Men, which I had later hidden in Missus Echolle's freezer behind her six month supply of butter. But it's unlikely because nobody knew where I lived.

"My poor husband is very near to the end of his tether. That was the very first train model he assembled!"

"Yea?"

"And also I should mention that they took your friend away for questions about her identity pass."

"What! They took Zi away?"

"Yes, but it is only a formality, do not worry; they will let her go. Now you should rest!"

"Yea, okay, goodnight," says I and it turns out to be a bloody lousy night for me. For starters I'm in pain and then I can't sleep a wink thinking about Zi and the bad bastards that had taken her away. By the time Missus Echolle calls me in the morning I'm very near to living in an hallucination. I don't really know what to do then, I don't know where Zi lives, and I think I was only dreaming that the da was in Baulox, so I take my granda's advice, which he says is the Dublin Work Motto: The best thing to do when you're up against it is to go on to work and pretend nothing has happened, no matter what size of a hangover you have, no matter what sort of trouble you're in.

I dress myself as best as I can with my spare clothes and take the bus to work.

Thirty-Four

Life goes on and so does the Works. Things haven't changed any, and as soon as I pass through the Kruxgoff security chute I'm surrounded by a horde of excitable gunmen who escort me up to Blumm's glasshouse. I'm starting to get used to the routine. Blumm himself doesn't look the best − in fact he looks completely shagged out and the wart on his nose has swelled up to the size of a strawberry. His missus must have been nagging at him again. And he must have been losing control of his brain too because the first thing he does is recite a poem to me:

"Ver Gazt vers dram gur scheidermunn gropt,
    Darf budderbucher antos howderflyster gezuminaff!
    Daf hiddillhostertweizer stopt
    Ver trans dikillslaft!"

"What?" says I. Baulox is bad enough but when you try and make poetry out of it you get some horrible sounding wogglewash.

"All our trials and tribulations!" says Blumm.

"I don't get you!"

"Never we mind. Hoofterkufterghoosh! Now, Herr Murphy, you are extremely aware that this very moment your father is presently in Baulox gutzleben."

"He's what?"

"You must understand your father's paternal concern having been in this city for ten whole days gutzleben in possession of a son with the audacity to escape without explanation from excellent medical treatment at night and hide away."

"I'm not hiding from anybody. Here I am on my way to work like anybody else."

"You must this very instance return into accomodation in the hospital in charge of competent medical authorities."

"I feel alright thanks."

Blumm is definitely not feeling great and I can't help thinking that maybe it's he who should go to hospital, for a wart operation, but I don't say anything about it. He shifts about in his oversized armchair like he has an itchy bum then, having got to an important decision, he presses one of the buttons on his desk. And in comes his secretary Manda who is looking like she is out for business in her zebra-striped shorts. On top she's wearing a blue and red bikini with some sort of strings hanging out of it.

"Now, Miss Zerinisky. This is the very man you have observed from the window at the hour of the unfortunate shooting incident in the top security sector?"

"That is correct, Herr Blumm. I observed Herr Murphy being shot down as he crossed the Zugzwang Line at Double B-Sector. At the time he looked very much like a child who had lost his way."

"Miss Zerinisky, let us forget poetic interference. Did he or did he not cross the Zugzwang Line?"

"Yes he did."

"The what?" says I.

"Daf Zugzwango buchaust von duf Klam Klam!" says Blumm getting narky.

"Oh, I wasn't supposed to go over there, was I?" says I. But Blumm won't answer me. He is getting more and more annoyed with himself, wriggling about in his armchair like an eel in a rowing boat, and trying to make his watch go faster. Obviously his wart is causing him big problems. Then he sends his secretary out again before I've time to let her know that I know she's a spy.

"You appear as very fortunate that events as viewed by Miss Zerinisky offer favourable repercussions for your case before Daf Tribunal."

"At what tribunal?"

"It is customary that all our employees are familiarised with the Works legal code; however, it has been brought to my notice that an oversight seems to have transpired to happen in your instance."

"I don't follow you," says I. The man is beginning to talk like Zuckermutter.

"You are aware, Herr Murphy, that the Works has not been built in one single day. So we have tradition, legal hoosterooge, dukswallopo and Daf Tribunal. All must be necessary to ensure a smooth running. Tistroff?"

"No, I don't understand why anyone should shoot me."

"Never we mind. That is not our very immediate problem. Doctor Grubbels has informed me that this is the very moment for you to be returned into the hospital."

"I feel fine thanks."

"Now, Herr Murphy, Doctor Grubbels is very much older with the heavy experience of years than what you are, and he has the information passed to me that following your operation you are suffering from a mental imbalance."

"What operation?" says I.

"Oh Schimmelblurger! Doctor Grubbels is by the standards of our times the most experienced consultant available in Baulox, East or West!"

"But I never even spoke to the man," says I.

"Oh gharst! Herr Murphy, your father is presently arriving here so I should suggest it will be in your very best interests to allow him make your decisions. For as I pointed out Doctor Grubbels has. . ."

"What! The da is coming here, is he?" So I wasn't dreaming after all.

"Please allow me to continue. . ." he says, but at that very moment there is a knock on the door and the da is shown in. Jazus! I can hardly believe the change in Blumm when the da arrives. He goes from being very nasty with a long narky puss to all smiles and gold teeth flashing all over the room. The da of course has the pipe in the mouth and the giant box of matches and I have to laugh at all the sparks flying over the carpet and puffy armchairs.

"Ah, welcome, Herr Murphy Senior! Sit yourself upon a seat! How is business in Dublin? Coffee will be gorterblacken in one moment or would you prefer our national Coko. I have only this instance being agreeably in conversation with your son."

"Thank you, Herr Blumm, but I won't have a drink. Against doctor's orders. My! What a stupendous view!"

"Yes indeed, Herr Murphy."

"I hope Paddy is taking it all in. I presume by the way that he is behaving himself?"

"As I have been saying, I have been conversing over a period with your son and is it clear as we say here in Baulox — jugsdown fluffersluft borkstein! — that your son has not awakened fully from the anaesthesia and must immediately be transported to return to the hospital."

"I see," says the da, taking a puff from the pipe.

"I'm wide awake," says I but they both ignore me.

"And of course, Herr Murphy, I expect you have been conversing with Doctor Grubbels and have arrived at the same conclusion as a result."

"Yes, Paddy is not cachectic, as he admits himself."

"A brilliant man is our Doctor Grubbels. One of our foremost consultants and a major diploma in vasectonomy, blursfluther and ghast!"

"Indeed, Herr Blumm! A man with a brilliantly exiguous mind!"

"A man of astute learning and method!"

"Yes, I suspect he used perfectly tendentious methods, and of course I noticed that he was very concerned about Paddy here," says the da, and throws me one of his meaningless glances.

"And I gather," continues the da, "that he is of the opinion that Paddy should be returned to the hospital."

"But, I feel fine da!" says I.

"Exactly, Herr Murphy! I am afraid that your son is at this moment unfortunate to be fhusterhopp and unable to portray his own predicament."

"Obviously not aphasic! And I understand your concern – a doctor is invariably his own worst patient. What would you yourself propose at this juncture, Herr Blumm?"

"There must be only one practical solution, Herr Murphy. Your son must return, ghusterhogger, immediately for continual medical treatments. In person otherwise I could not be responsible, tistroff?"

"I see. I expect Paddy will take the pusillanimous course and agree to that suggestion now that his nocturnal adventures are over. Would that be correct, Paddy?"

"No, I don't want to go back to hospital," says I.

"Michael," says Blumm, calling the da by his first name, "it is one of the wonders of modermilche medicine that even sick persons, jeusterbolle, can delude themselves in their thoughts that they are in a fine fettle of health, so your son should return his body into the hospital or we might not forgive the consequences."

"Yes indeed, Herr Blumm! The body is a very complicated affair, not at all as simple as a mere machine, a bicycle for example."

"Ah ha! Daf boofshitter!" says Blumm.

"Which reminds me," says the da giving me a dark look. "Paddy, I caught that insouciant friend of yours in flagrante delicto!"

"What?" says I.

"The bicycle," continues the da, "takes only relatively elementary prognosis and diagnosis."

"What are you taking about?" says I.

"Yes Michael, so the proposition I propose to make is that you should sign this form here on behalf of your son. Doctor Grubbels has very

124

kindly had it escorted here to allow an immediate return for your son. The hospital is at a natural reluctance to allow embarrassment in this matter, however Doctor Grubbels has very kindly pointed to the solution where the parent may take control of the son's body by placing a signature on this form.''

"Indeed," says the da, "Doctor Grubbels struck me as a most inquiring consultant – a lugubrious gentleman if I may say so. Not a harsh word did he use against Paddy here after his rebellious behaviour. He almost gave me the indication that he would be keen to have him back."

"The certain sign of a professional, Michael. Never at a satisfaction until the problem has been eradicated."

"Precisely! Now we won't waste any more of your valuable time. If you just give me over the form we will. . . ''

"Here you are, Michael, all you must do is sign underneath."

"Excellent," says the da picking up the form, folding it and putting it away in his inside pocket.

"Now come along, Paddy, there is a taxi waiting outside," he says.

"Really, Michael, I can save you a burden of difficulty. I had made an anticipation of your decision, ghoosterhobb, and so the ambulance is waiting outside on the alert, which will no doubt be at service to both your avail for the return to hospital."

"That is very considerate, but I would not allow that. If Paddy has the audacity to remove himself under his own steam, he can damn well suffer the consequences and return the same way. Now come along, Paddy!''

And I had been sure the da was going to sign me down the Swurge River. He just doesn't seem to be aware that the Baulox Hospital is a dangerous place. On the way out to the taxi he gets into a big curiosity about everything in the Works, asking me all sorts of questions. What is that? How does that work? What are those men doing (Deb Flustes)? Why is there a revolving cupola on top of that laminated tower? And he doesn't stop with the questions until we're aboard the taxi and pissing down the Baulox Highway. Only then does he offer an opinion.

"Very advanced!" he says.

"Yea?"

"Very advanced!" he repeats.

"I suppose so," says I.

"Tell me, Paddy, what's behind that long black wall running along the road?''

"Oh, that is the Goosshitch Area where all the nuclear stations melted away."

"Very advanced!" says the da.

"Yea?" says I. I'm not really interested, and thinking more about how I'm going to convince him not to take me to the hospital.

Thirty-Five

As we get to the Baulox Flyover I let the da know I don't want him to take me to the hospital.

"Paddy," he says, "I have no intention of taking you anywhere. How old are you now?"

"Seventeen," says I.

"Well, that is old enough for you to make your own decisions. Napoleon could hardly have been much older when he won his first battle. I found it quite unseemly, Paddy, that a son of mine should act like an adolescent whippersnapper in the presence of a man of Herr Blumm's social standing. You should display the utmost deference to his suggestions notwithstanding the fact that you may or may not intend to carry out a different course of action to the one he prescribes. If you don't wish to go to hospital that is your own business. . . and unfortunately mine also."

"Blumm would have carted me off to the hospital if you hadn't got a taxi."

"Taradiddle, Paddy, absolute tosh! Only an obsequious idiot would allow himself to be incarcerated in a hospital against his wishes."

"Sure, Jazus, hadn't he an ambulance parked outside the front door."

"Driver! Take a left down there," says the da.

"But da, you're taking us right into the heart of the West Sector."

"Good. Now what were we saying? Oh yes, about ambulances, vehicles with blue and red lights protruding from the roof. That was merely in the eventuality of your needing such a vehicle."

"But da, there's nothing over here except Flesh Clubs and that sort of thing."

"Paddy, you should remember the maxim from Rome: When in Rome. . .!"

"But we're not in Rome!"

"Oh, stop quibbling. Now driver, stop there! I should imagine we should get a good strong cup of coffee in that restaurant across the road."

"Da, that's the Bokkoblooster Club! It's meant to be one of the worst joints in the city!"

"It certainly looks respectable from the outside. What is so offputting about its interior, Paddy?"

"Well, I haven't been inside myself but I heard. . ."

"Now, Paddy! I'm astonished that you should place such credence in mere rumours."

There is no talking to the man at all. He drags me into the Bokkoblooster Club which has a big reputation for being very notorious. Of course, being with the da makes me feel nothing can go wrong.

Two fat-bellied bouncers dressed up in black and white harlequin uniforms get us to sign our names in the visitors' book and we go downstairs to the lounge. Naturally I think the da, him being a practising catholic who plays chess with the parish priest, will walk straight out of there. There's some sort of orgy going on, but the da doesn't seem to notice — he goes straight over to where the naked women are with the bananas and whips and sits himself down on a large purple sofa. Why all the women are eating bananas is anybody's guess.

"Will we try somewhere else, da?" says I.

"Not at all, Paddy, this will do fine. Would you signal one of those young girls to come over."

"Hey! You!" says I.

"My, my, Paddy, they are not donkeys, do you want us to be thrown out of here? Excusee moy bonney momazella!" says the da and one of the women with the whips comes straight over to him.

"Ballzimmer gortstopper offill fump drubber am gumm slift!?" she calmly asks, and it's only then that I learn the da can speak perfectly good Baulox.

"Gadstructorf, vist amput klokore blackermacken nuk globser!" he says and she glances over at me as if to say this request for beef sandwiches and coffee is outrageous. The da has to cajole her a bit.

"Umm brassick!" he says. He always had a soft heart for the mustard, although by the time she returns with the tray I bet he must have forgotten he was hungry because things are starting to hot up as the women put their clients through their paces. One particular prominent politician sitting near us had rashly ordered five women with whips and from the sounds he is making, I'd guess he is going to fade off into the next life. But the da doesn't seem to hear them moaning.

"Excellent sandwiches but the coffee is rather tepid," he says.

"Yea? But I'm not hungry. Would you mind eating mine?"

"Now, Paddy! Are you not feeling well? Perhaps we should go straight to the hospital?"

"No, it's just that it's a bit stuffy in here."

"Nonsense, Paddy, now take off your jacket and eat up those sandwiches."

"What d'ye think of this place?"

"As I said, Paddy, the coffee is rather tepid. Tell me, what is that purple liquid everyone is imbibing?"

"Oh that's called Morschnort! A brandy of sorts."

"Well, we shall try a carafe. Excusee moy bonney momazella!"

"But da, it's fairly deadly stuff!"

"Now, Paddy, as the good Lord himself says. . ."

Thirty-Six

Wham! There comes a horrible big blank now because I don't want to remember much more after that. After the da gets a whiff of the Morschnort things go peculiar awful. He develops a fierce addiction for the stuff.

"An excellent vintage!" he keeps on saying and the two of us get cross-eyed elephants. Several of the women with the whips and bananas get themselves involved with us — word games and whatnot and then one of them produces a deck of cards. That sort of thing, but I don't remember too much until I wake up the following morning in the da's hotel bedroom. I'm in his bed and he is in an armchair reading the *Baulox Press*. There are empty bottles of Morschnort all over the place.

"Where are we?" says I but he doesn't answer.

"Hey da! Are you alright?"

I may as well be talking to a spaceman. He's asleep and only pretending to be reading the paper. I take the paper out of his face and while I'm taking a glance through it, at the usual stories about dangerous gorillas who should be locked up, I come across my girlfriend's name on the third page — Zi Garift. That stops me in my tracks. I read:

Zi Garift and Petro Hoofnet, two prominent members of the illegal LLL Assembly are to appear before the terrorist tribunal today at four o'clock. The army are making special security arrangements (hogmokker donk orghanizationaliset duuurt) for the trial.

Forgetting all about the da I leave the hotel and take myself in a big hurry across the city to The Harbour Bar. I don't quite know what to do but I must make a plan of some sort to get her out of prison or wherever she is. The first thing I need is a gun and I'm hoping Missus Echolle hasn't thrown my gun away.

She has thrown it away so I lock myself into my room and try and figure out a plan. It's not all that easy although I've seen hundreds of guys do it in the pictures and then I read about it once in a book. The man in the book got himself the best bottle of whisky ever made in Scotland and poured it out by measuring his fingers, and by doing this he was able to stay in the hotel until the right moment. After measuring four of his fingers, he carefully cleaned his gun, burnt a piece of paper, measured another finger, walked across to the courtroom, and at that very moment it just happened that his girlfriend who he was trying to rescue was bursting for a piss (although later she turned out to be a baddie – she had only been pretending to work for the American Busman's Union when in fact she was working for the Chinese Voodoo Society), so all the hero had to do was point the gun at the lavatory attendant and away they went in an antique car with a super-modern engine in it. Then out of the blue they were followed by a man with a false face in a modern blue sportscar, but to everyone's amazement their car was faster than his, and the man with the false face couldn't understand it, and then they lost him altogether on the back road to Monto Gubi where the man with the false face drove off a cliff on a bad bend.

The problem is it's not that easy to think up a plan as smart as that, and all I can think of is going to see Kamam of the LLL and tell him I want my girlfriend out of prison. So I leave The Harbour Bar and head in the general direction of the slums; that's where I had last met Kamam, in 50B Flapp Street. At least I haven't forgotten the address.

It's hard to find the slums because they are hidden away somewhere at the back of the Pervo Centres and the Flesh Clubs. I ask several people for directions but once they hear the word slums (HOOFGAPTER) they back away from me like I'm a mad polar bear. In the end I have to get help from one of the bouncers at the doorway of a middle-class Flesh Club. He's a big brute of a man who looks at me as if he's intending to smash my jaw, then he waves a large hairy fist at the sky: "Gluglorst Horkenswid! (Straight on!)" he says.

"Thanks," says I, wondering does he think I have an aircraft, and walk on and around in a few circles, and just when I'm thinking of collapsing on the pavement, I see the slums. These are a load of grey and brown boxes piled in on top of one another where all the people with no jobs live. They have been parked down in a valley behind a big smokescreen so that prominent politicians and important people won't see them. According to the *Baulox Press* the slum dwellers spend all their money on shagg, tobacco, and the Pools, and they don't like working in factories.

First prize in the Pools (Daf Humpbox) is a staggering fifty million Kacks, and if you were to believe the press every second Bauloxonion had won billions. Of course, Zi told me this was all nonsense. Now and again they gave a prize to some lunatic who would buy a fast car and kill himself so that all the money would go flying back fast into the Baulox Exchequer. I'm hardly at the edge of the slums when I'm approached by a Pools salesman with a limp. He won't let me by.

"Daf Humpbox!" he keeps on saying, so I have to buy twenty Kacks worth. A big smile comes on his face when he sees the colour of my money and he hands me over some very impressive looking documents with loads of highly official Baulox Exchequer writing on them. What with a bit of luck, I'm thinking, I might even become a Baulox millionaire.

"Where is Flapp Street?" I ask him in Baulox and he directs me to Block H. It's about five minutes away and is the replica of all the other buildings – cracked! With a bad smell of dog piss and burning banana skins, smashed windows, kids playing with ropes and fat women bursting off the balconies. I'm climbing up the stone stairway and who do I meet only Kamam himself coming out of a toilet on the third floor with a big cigar in his mouth.

"Kamam! Just the man I'm looking for!" says I, and Holy Missus Maloney! I never saw a man move so fast. He goes skidding around the corner like a kitten with a boot on his tail, and straight out through a fire exit. I run after him but he's gone.

"Come back!" says I to myself. And I'm waiting there like a terrible eejit not knowing what to do until I decide to go on up to 50B on the next floor. I give a rap on the door thinking nobody will answer, but next minute it opens and I'm dragged inside and forced onto the ground. A big shoe is placed awkwardly on my stomach and I find Kamam and three other unfriendly faces from the love movement glaring down at me. Skinnyface with the greasy blonde hair opens the conversation.

"Vastukupter naranski adar forl?" (Who are you?)

"Vastukupter naranski skerdan?" (Who sent you?)

All very well if I can answer back but the breath has been kicked out of me and all I can do is gurgle for air. And then suddenly they relax themselves a bit because Kamam recognises me. He reaches immediately for the box of cigars.

"It was you from Ireland who promised to assist us capture Daf Einfanb. Have a cigar, they are the best available."

"No thanks, I came to see what you were going to do about Zi and the other fellah."

"Ah! Petro Hoofnet! And Zi Garift! You have come at the right time — but first, how did you know where our Headquarters were?"

"Headquarters?"

"Answer!"

"See that envelope over there on the table: that was there when I was here last, and it gives this address."

"Ah! So you are observant, what no? And now we are planning a Zungerbloost!"

"A what?"

"A war conference, perhaps we may allow you sit in on it. It is against regulations yet we are nearly ready now for open takeover and liberation!"

"Good, then you can let Zi out of jail."

Thirty-Seven

Daf Zungerbloost and orders to return to work to help capture Daf Einfanb. Herr Windtail loses one of his contact lenses and Jody comes over suff zur telesplopper!

It's the first war conference I was ever at. Very complicatory. First the room is filled up with cigar smoke while the maps are spread around the war desk. Kamam removes his binoculars. He points to the map. A pin is stuck in it. Then things start getting under way: the first job on the agenda is the liberation of the prisoners from the courthouse.

Bumweiner who is the tall fellah with the golf ball imprint on his forhead − seems there was some kind of accident when his mother abandoned him on a golf course − is given the job of rounding up a few men, waylaying an army patrol, derobing the soldiers, locking them up naked in the Berovski Sewer, and proceeding to the courthouse dressed up as a Baulox captain. There he is to assassinate the three judges and the witnesses for the prosecution. And Kamam says he should know what to do himself after that.

Bushybeard whose name I don't know has an easier task. He is to hang around the Terrorist Tribunal Building and keep Kamam up with the developments by using Code 4, whatever that is.

Skinnyface with the blond hair and the big shoes is to cause a small diversion by blowing up the Waterworks and a few sets of traffic lights. And that's it.

"What about me?" says I.

"You are ordered to work to help capture Daf Einfanb."

"But I want to help."

"But nothing. That is an order. You'll have to obey orders."

"Me and Jody and the lads don't take orders."

"You will have to learn. The security of this State depends on us."

There is no talking to this Kamam fallah at all and he doesn't want me to do anything except get Daf Einfanb. I leave then with a terrible hangover from all the drinking with the da, and the cigar smoke. I jump on the first bus that comes by and get into the Works at God knows what hour of the day. This time the gunmen let me proceed on down to Q-Sector where I find a big uproar taking place. Herr Windtail has dropped one of his contact lenses on the floor and all work has stopped.

The men are down on their knees crawling about looking for it and Windtail nearly goes a seizure when I arrive.

"Nak gampt gistertrochersnult!" he roars. (Don't move!)

"What's up?" says I.

"Moo sunblishter!" he roars.

"Oh, you lost your lens again," says I, and I'm about to join the search when I hear my name come over the loudspeaker.

"Herr Paddy Murphy sugafta suff zur telesplopper!" (I'm wanted on the phone.)

"Yea?" says I into the phone. I'm thinking it must be the da. I'd have to do something about him – get him back to Dublin before he loses his religion with all the Morschnort and what not.

"Hello, put me onto Paddy Murphy, this is urgent!"

"Hallo?" says I "Who is that?"

"Listen," says the voice on the other end, "this is my fourth telephone call, and if you don't put me onto Mister Murphy there'll be hell to pay."

"I am Paddy Murphy."

"Well, Jazus, about time, my old flower."

"Who's that?"

"Who do you think! Are your ears acting up on you?"

"It couldn't be Jody?"

"It couldn't be anyone else, could it? D'ye think it's Santy Claus?"

"I don't believe it! Who's letting you phone up from Dublin?"

"Dublin me eye! I'm phoning from the pub up the road. Are you coming out for a pint?"

"Who's with you? How did. . ."

"Are you coming or aren't you!"

"I'm at work here. . ."

"I know where you are, and I'm in the first pub past the airport, so get on your bicycle and come on over."

"What's the name of the pub?"

"How in the Jazus would I know what it's called, it's written up in ducktalk foreign. But you can't miss it, it's the first pub past the airport! And there's a carpark outside with a plastic oak tree in it."

"Okay, I'll see you out there in a few minutes," says I.

"Right!" says Jody and puts down the phone. And for a while I can hardly believe it. Jody who has never been outside Ireland in his life is in Baulox!

Thirty-Eight

THE FIRST PUB PAST THE AIRPORT AND FUCKING SHAGG! THE STORY ABOUT
GAME DUCK, IRISH TRAITORS, THE KOOFNOR BAR, THE HUMVOX
BAR. . . THE HOMMERSTOKER TAVERNA. 5 GOWFFER GUTZWANKT ZUM
TRIBUNALE MISINTRORRE DORTSHAT. AND OBLIVION.

When the dinner hooter blasts off I dash out of the Works and grab the
bus into the city. I'm in a fierce state of wanting to be in the pub with
Jody at the same time as I'm on the bus. I can't wait to get there and
maybe that's why the bus takes so long to get anywhere near the airport.

Jody is in Baulox! What a turn up for the comics! Jody is the best
friend I've ever had, and although some people think he's a bit touched,
like his head wasn't put on right in the hospital, he's as sane as the next
man. The neighbours at home are inclined to think that just because his
father is an extreme extrovert who solves all his problems in the pub and
always arrives home pissed and smashes up the crockery and has ferocious
slanging matches with his missus in the bedroom, that Jody is the same.
But Jody is different!

Jody is his own boss and never does what he's told. And he doesn't
look like anybody I know — he's shorter than me, curly black hair with
hawk eyes that are always grinning, a broken nose in four places, and one
and a half cracked teeth up front which happened when he somersault-
ed over the handlebars of the bicycle coming down Howth Hill without
back brakes. Jody had captured a black headed gull and was bringing him
home to have as a pet when the front brakes turned his bike into an
aeroplane. It was the funniest thing I'd ever seen until I saw all the blood
on the road.

I'm thinking about this and other things we used to do together
while I'm trying to find the first pub past the airport. It seems to take me
an age and I feel about four years older by the time I get there. Of course,
I can't miss the place because of the plastic oak tree, one of the daftest
things I've ever seen, and then the pub is packed out the door like there
was a race meeting on across the road, and there's a tremendous sound of
excitement coming from inside. When I push my way in I find Jody
roaring his head off at a table in the centre of the pub. And some of the
lads are with him. Micko the liberator, who was born in a fuse box, is
there. Hairlips, who wrote me a letter and never says more words than

necessary, is there. Stabber O'Neill, who is an alcoholic and learning how to be a sign painter, is there. Pidgeon McGrath, who is an alcoholic, is there. And of course the Bauloxonions are there, standing around gaping at Jody and the lads like they were something out of a zoo.

They are singing a bit of a song that Jody's granny wrote. Jody is lead singer, Micko is playing drums with two empty glasses, Pidgeon is playing through a dirty comb, and Stabber is generally making as much noise as possible. A tremendous sound and much better than anything in the Baulox Hit Parade. The words are highly polished and unique:

"WE JUST ESCAPED, WE JUST ESCAPED, WE JUST ESCAPED, FROM THE LOONEY BIN, FROM THE LOONEY BIN, AND WE'RE FREE, COS WE'RE FREE, COS WE'RE FREE, COS THEY COULDN'T KEEP US IN, HURRAH! HURRAH! O'LEARY, McDONOGH, PADDY TYNAM AND ME. . ."

And just then Jody sees me. He stops the song in mid-air and lets out an unholy shout: "Murphy! How are ye!"

"What're you having, Paddy?" asks Pidgeon who always likes to drink in rounds.

"They've no pints here. Only little glasses!" says Stabber.

"Where are the rest of the lads?" says I.

"They couldn't all afford to come over – we had to leave Gus, Tarzan Brown, Boots Cassidy and the rest of them at home."

"I'll have a brandy and shagg!" says I.

"Brandy and what?" says Jody.

"Shagg!"

"Fucking shagg! Eh? So that's what the world is coming to!"

"Alright, shaggs all around," says Pidgeon.

"How'd ye get over here?" says I.

"It's a long story!" says Jody.

It's some story alright! What happened was that Hairlips got a tip straight from the bitch's mouth, a dog called Game Duck. He was out one night drinking with the trainer's missus.

"What trainer?" says I.

"How would I know?" says Jody. "Some wagon he met in Bill's."

It turned out she was the woman in the know anyway and she told Lips to keep an eye out for the next time it was running. God's honour!

For some reason Game Duck hadn't been going at full speed before –
something to do with what they were giving him to eat: soggy
cornflakes. They kept pulling him back some way. But God's honour!
They started feeding him up on steak and the next time he got onto a race
track he was going to go at a queer gallop.

So when Lips told Jody, Jody told Micko to cash in his Life Savings
Bonds which his granduncle had left him, and for a whole week they
were watching the paper like hawks for a sign of Game Duck. It looked
bad for a while because they were drinking away their life savings but
then Game Duck popped into the paper saying he was going off in the
8.55 at Harold's Cross on the Friday, and before they knew it they had
ten or eleven times as much money as they ever had in their life, and
nothing to do with it except go out to the airport and get tickets to
Baulox where they had heard the crack was ninety-ninety point nine.
And there they were in the first pub past the airport.

Where, after plenty of brandy and shaggs, things start getting out of
hand. We're all a bit pissed and enjoying ourselves, but the Bauloxon-
ions don't like it. They start getting ferocious serious watching us all the
time with disapprovals stamped on their faces.

"Listen lads," says I. "We'd better calm things down a bit. They
might call in the army!"

Jody seems to think this is a big joke. "Call in the army!" (And
then he roars laughing.)

"Serious!" says I.

"They can call in the American Washerwoman's Assocation for all I
care," says he.

"It's not like back in Dublin."

"I thought the crack was ninety over here!"

"Well, they don't like you singing."

"Then they can go and fuck off with themselves!" says Jody, and he
calls for a big hush then because he's going to organise a recital of the
song 'Irish Traitors' that his second cousin's uncle wrote in the mental
hospital during the war. And I wonder what the reception is going to be
– this cousin's uncle was famous in Dublin for having been barred out
of twenty-seven pubs in one day for trying to render this song.

"Shush!" says Jody. "We are now going to sing that well known
song wrote by my cousin's uncle when he was a prisoner in his country
during the war. It's called 'Irish Traitors'! Are you ready lads!"

It's hard to write down music but the song goes something like this
– The Bauloxonions stand around very perplexed –

138

WE DON'T LIKE SOLDIERS OR FUCKING SAILORS
Pidgeon starts playing the comb, Micko bangs out the beat.
WHO LOCK US AWAY IN THOSE ASYLUMS
Everybody stamp their feet.
WE DON'T LIKE JUDGES OR FUCKING JAILORS!
Let out continual whoopees!

WE DON'T LIKE THEIR LORDS AND FUCKING LADIES
Turn up volume!
WE DON'T LIKE THEIR LAWS AND FISHING WARDENS
Cheer!
THOSE FUCKING SOLDIERS AND FUCKING SAILORS!
Roar out this line!

WE DO TIME, THEY CALL US BLEEDING WASTERS
Chorus go booh!
THEY SEND US DOWN WITHOUT ANY REASON
Chorus say yeah!
THOSE FUCKING JUDGES AND FUCKING JAILORS!
Scream out this line!

THEY'RE ONLY A CROWD OF IRISH TRAITORS
Serious foot stomp! Bang glasses!
THOSE FUCKING SCREWS WHO PATROL THEIR PRISONS
Chorus shout anything that comes to mind
THOSE FUCKING SOLDIERS AND FUCKING SAILORS!
Start breaking one or two glasses.

WE DON'T LIKE THEIR SCHOOLS OR LACKEY TEACHERS
Roar!
WHO TEACH US ENGLISH THROUGHOUT ALL SEASONS
Scream!
AND ACT LIKE PREACHERS AND FUCKING JAILORS!
Scream!   Roar!   Up volume!

TAKE UP YOUR AXES AND FUCKING RAZORS
Roar out this line.
TAKE DOWN YOUR PIKES AND KNIVES AND WEAPONS
Break a couple more glasses.
WE DON'T LIKE SOLDIERS AND FUCKING SAILORS

Up beat for last line
AND FUCKING DOCTORS AND FUCKING JAILORS!
And stop suddenly!

And there follows an astonished silence in the bar. Several Bauloxon-ions make towards the telephones and I think even Jody senses that they are going to call in the army. I see him giving Micko a nudge and slanting his head over towards the door.

"Must be a better pub than this around," he says.

"Load of them," says I, and we slip out quick and quietly and go off on a pub crawl making sure to stay off the main airport road. The Koofnor Bar. . .The Humvox. . .Daf Doorschnotter. Pidgeon doesn't find this kip amenable so we track off to Daf Juggleschnorter which is a better bar by far. Jody and the lads are going wild singing and having the crack, but for some reason I'm not really enjoying it. Maybe I'm tired or pissed off or something because half the time I can't catch the jokes. And maybe it's because my head is full up with Daf Einfanb and the LLL and Zi, and the Eight Sane Men, and the da, and it's enough to drive me up the walls.

And then I lose the lads altogether in the Hooftvokker Palace. One minute they're there and another they've left. I am talking to some geezer from Baulox at the bar about the Pools at the time and I haven't a clue where they've got themselves to. Soon I'm wandering all over the back streets of Baulox looking for them, and then of all people I bump into the da in the Hommerstoker Taverna. He's sitting up at the plastic counter drinking and reading the late edition of the *Baulox Press*. It's funny but he neither looks surprised or glad to see me.

"Well, Paddy! Are you off work already?"

"Took the day off. Tell me, did you see Jody or any of the lads around?"

"I certainly did not! Have those hooligans come over here? Now, if I know anything, Paddy, they should be left to their own devices."

"It's the other way around. They have left me to my own devices. I haven't a clue where they've got to."

"You can count your blessings and mark my words — as soon as they land themselves in hot water which they undoubtedly will, you will hear from them. Whether you are aware of it or not, you have held down a responsible job with one of the most powerful firms in the city for some months now, and as such you must wield considerable influence. Which

140

reminds me that you are due for a vacation and perhaps we may arrange to leave for Dublin tomorrow morning.''

''No I can't, sure there's too much going on now, they've locked up my girlfriend and God knows what else.''

''Paddy, that is the most opportune time to leave, when things are preying on your mind. . .''

He is beginning to talk hot wogglewash just like he does at home until a fine looking young one breezes into the bar, comes straight over to the da, kisses him on the ear and then sits down beside him. Jazus! The da must be pushing seventy if he hasn't gone over it, and this young blondey one is no more than sixteen. Or seventeen at the most. And not wearing enough clothes for a four year old. All she has on is a short black dress with a large zipper running down the centre of it with a big gold ring at the top. You'd be very tempted to give the ring a good pull and then she'd have nothing at all on.

''Orsa!'' says the da. ''Let me introduce you to my son Paddy who has been employed in Baulox for almost six months now at the Works. Orsa like myself works in the Civil Service and we have been making some rudimentary comparisons between our system and theirs.''

''So this is your son about which you have spoken so often to me. How charming!''

''How'ye!'' says I. ''Da, would you give us a look at that rag you have there?''

''Certainly, Paddy. What would you like to drink, Orsa?''

''Christ!'' says I for I've seen something on the front page of the paper that makes my heart skip.

''Pardon me, Paddy?''

5   GOWFFER   GUTZWANKT   ZUM   TRIBUNALE MINISTRORRE DORTSHAT! (Probably about twenty judges and five terrorists slain in court siege!)

''Will you have a drink, Paddy?''

''No, no it doesn't matter,'' says I. My eyes are blurring and I can hardly read the paper. My hands are shaking. And then I gulp hard suddenly, for the very first victim's name is Zi Garift. . .

"Are you alright, Paddy?"

"No, I'm alright," says I, dropping the paper and making for the door. There follows a long walk.

I go the length and breadth of Baulox and a poisoned veil of depression covers it all. Zi was gone. It only seems like now I can see her for what she was – just a young girl caught up with politics. And I'm thinking maybe she needed my help and I can't give it now. My hands clench and tears force themselves out, but I don't care. I don't care about anything. Her face is remarkably clear but I can't talk to her, touch her. . .O. . .Lost. And what was it for? It all? The system. The stupid armies, the LLL. Love my arse. It's all useless. Doesn't mean anything. Nothing. Advertisements all over the city glare at me. Sun-bronzed cowboys smoking cigarettes. Butter. Something to do with white teeth and sponge cake. Fucking bananas. Milk! Athletes jumping over a stream. Rubbish. Chocolate. Shit! What we make of everything. What they make. Mad, everything is mad and everyone is going around unhappy, miserable, distorting their faces, hiding from one another, behind masks, behind curtains, behind car doors, walls, everywhere. I don't care how mad I look. Hands, bits of hands, fingers and tits and bums and confusion, watches, clocks, fear, all wrapped up in a swirl of concrete and metal pipes twisting up and away to nowhere. And Zi is dead. Murdered!

I can't think and I know I'm walking all over the place. I nearly get knocked down by a car, and then somehow I meet Jody but it's only a dream. Surely God it's a dream. It's got to be. Jody keeps on talking to me. I don't know what, and then there's a bed. Must be in Dublin, and then I fall and sort of disappear into oblivion.

Thirty-Nine

TAKING A VAN LOAD OF SAUSAGES TO THE WEST PERIMETER OF THE GOOSSHITCH AREA, AND DECIDING TO GET THE BLAZES OUT OF BAULOX ON THE FIRST FLIGHT WE CAN GET OUR HANDS ON.

Even oblivion doesn't last forever, for I wake up in my room in The Harbour Bar to find the lads kipping on the floor and Jody sitting on the side of the bed, a big grin on his face and a bottle of whisky in his hand.

"What are you grinning at?" says I.

"At yourself and your bombs!" says Jody.

"What bombs?"

"Didn't you keep us awake half the night with your plan to steal the Vital Ingredient for the bomb."

"First I heard of it."

"Murphy, you're cracking up. Here, have a drink and calm your nerves. This is the plan we made last night!"

He hands me a dirty big piece of cardboard with a lot of stuff and diagrams written on it. And some of it's in my writing.

"Although, I was sorry to hear about your girlfriend," says Jody.

"Did I tell you about that?"

"You told us it all. Now you'd better get out of bed because we're knocking off this Vital Ingredient tonight."

"We're what?"

"Hey lads! Time to get up!" shouts Jody.

It's some plan! It hinges on the fact that Micko is an apprentice electrician who served some of his time and spent six weeks getting the technical side of it in the University of Bolton Street. Him and Hairlips are going to cut off the whole electricity supply to the Works and surrounding areas. Nothing simpler, he says, as long as he gets a very good hacksaw with a rubber handle and spare blades.

Part B of the plan is that Stabber and Pidgeon clean up the loose ends and make sure they get us all tickets for the aeroplane and keep an eye on things at The Harbour Bar, and being alcoholics they should be well able for this.

Part C is that Jody and me have to knock off a van, wait for the lights to go out and drive in through the Goosshitch Area where all the old stations melted away, break into BB-Sector and steal the Essential (or

Vital as Jody calls it) Ingredient for the bomb while the Klam Klam alarm has been shut up.

Part D is we escape with Daf Einfanb in the van and we all meet up in The Harbour Bar.

And the last part of it is that we hand the bomb over to the LLL and get to blazes out of there on the first flight.

Before we set about it Missus Echolle makes us all breakfast and it's good fun because Jody and her get on like a fizz bag and a liquorice pipe. Even Mister Echolle enjoys himself because Pidgeon knows something about model aeroplanes. When Pidgeon was seven years old he suffered from a bad doctor and had to spend eight months in bed making model aircraft. Seems that the doctor spent all his time sticking needles up Pidgeon's arse and only when the doctor was called away to start another emergency did he get better. It's the best breakfast I've ever been at and immediately afterwards we set to work.

Micko and Lips go off to steal some electrical gear and a hacksaw because even with all our winnings and the money the soldiers gave away we only have enough for air tickets. Jody and me go off to steal a van. And Stabber and Pidgeon stay on at The Harbour Bar to keep the custom going.

We're only away about ten minutes when we come across just the job outside one of the hypermarkets. It's a plain blue van with back doors open and the man who works for it having gone off into the butcher compartment of the shop with a big tray of sausages.

"This'll do the trick!" says Jody.

"There's a rake of sausages in it," says I.

"That doesn't matter, close the back doors there and we'll be off."

It's as simple as that and Jody doesn't even have to use his magic key to liberate it. We drive back towards The Harbour Bar.

"He might get the traffic police after us," says I.

"No he won't," says Jody. "He'll think he parked it somewhere else. He won't want to make an eejit out of himself over a van load of sausages, and anyway we'll get Stabber to paint a sign up on it. Stabber's going to be one of the best signwriters in Dublin if he can hold his gargle."

"Never thought of that," says I.

Soon as we get back Jody gets him out from the bar with a couple of Mister Echolle's paint brushes and tells him to make a sign on the van that makes it look like thousands of others in the city and change the colour a bit and a few of the numbers.

"Bob's me uncle's landlady," says Stabber but he has to get assistance from me because he doesn't grasp the language. It seems to me that the best thing to put on it is BAULOX FLISTERSLOOSH (Baulox Cleaners) because there's hundreds of them, different colours and shapes, and what they're all cleaning I don't know. And believe it or don't believe it but Stabber turns out to be a dab hand at the job – he makes very square letters and beautiful straight lines better than I could do with a ruler.

Micko and Hairlips don't have it so easy and it's almost two hours before they come back in a state of excitement after having nearly been caught redhanded stealing a spade. But they have the gear with them – spade, clippers, screwdrivers, hammers, saws and a few other odds and ends that Micko said might come in useful. It's no use without the right tools was Micko's granda's policy.

After that there isn't all that much to do, we take our time getting things right, have one or two last drinks, synchronise the watches like they do in the war comics, pile into the van, all except Pidgeon and Stabber, and drive down the Baulox Highway. We dump Lips and Micko in a quiet spot between the New Nuclear Station and the Works at the backside of a marmalade advertisement. Couldn't be a better spot according to Micko because the pipes go under the road there.

"See youz back in the local," says Jody.

"Yea, and don't forget to liberate that bomb!" shouts Micko after us as we drive off to do a survey of the Goosshitch Area. We park the van outside a scrapyard on the West Perimeter of the Goosshitch Fence where we can just about see Blumm's glasshouse sticking over the Works. And then there's nothing to do except wait for the dark and the lads to switch off the electrics.

"This'll do fine!" says Jody. "The fence looks weak there, we'll just snip it open a bit and drive straight through it when the lights go out."

Forty

The Goosshitch Area! Bad Fish, that's what it is. It's like something out of a very ill imagination, like a place you'd expect to find on somebody else's planet after they had abandoned it because of a plague. Inside the huge electric fence which runs around the West Perimeter of the area are piles of old storage tanks, empty warehouses, and a big tangle of giant concrete pipes, and a lot of purplish moss growing up the sides of them. All along the fence are big red and yellow signs: DIEKUNCT! NUK STROFFER! (Keep the Jazus out of here!)

"What happened in there anyway?" says Jody.

"How would I know?"

"I mean, what were they trying to do in there?"

"Make electricity as far as I know," says I.

"Must have made a balls of it!" says Jody.

"Yea, it's a bit weird."

"It's a whole lot weird."

"I think some of the stations melted away," says I.

"Must have done something stupid. And it's funny but I don't understand them too well."

"How d'ye mean?"

"I mean, why do they need so many lights? Even in that pub we were in with the plastic oaktree – lights everywhere, even on the tree."

"Brightens up things I suppose," says I.

"Ah! It just blinds out everything else so you can't see it."

"Yea, I suppose so."

"Nuts," says Jody.

"Yea."

"We're a long way from the North Strand."

"I know. Why did you come over here anyway?" says I.

"Yea, I was meaning to ask you, Murphy – what's been getting into your old man lately?"

"I don't know, he started acting up a bit queer when he arrived in Baulox."

"Oh yea, somebody was telling me he arrived over here, came into The Harbour Bar looking for you last night but you weren't there. No,

146

but I wasn't meaning that — before he ever came over here. I mean he wouldn't even let me borrow my own bicycle to go around the corner to put on a bet.''

"He thinks it's his."

"Yea, but even apart from that — he won't scarcely say a word to me, and then what's all this telling the lads to write to you and ask you to come home?''

"How would I know? Maybe he's suffering from old age?"

"I don't know," says Jody.

"What else?"

"I mean, he never struck me as thick if you get my meaning."

"No, not thick, stupid maybe," says I.

"No, Murphy, it's more he never lets on what he's thinking, not like you.''

"How d'ye mean not like me."

"You couldn't look a cripple in the face without asking him what's wrong with his foot.''

"What's wrong with that?"

"Ah, Jazus, I'm not saying there's something wrong with it, but your old man would go around it another way.''

"How would he do it?"

"Now if I knew that I'd hardly be asking you — he'd say something different.''

"How would he?"

"Okay, he'd say something like — I don't like, or he wouldn't even say that, he'd say — I don't care too much for that shopkeeper across the way because I can't look the man straight in the eye!''

"And what's that got to do with a crippled foot?" says I.

"Because there's nothing wrong with the cripple's eyes — it's the shopkeeper then that turns out to be the cripple.''

"You're starting to talk, Jody, like Herr Zuckermutter!''

"Who the fuck is Huckershutter?"

"Just a guy I work with."

"Well anyway, Paddy, I just wanted to tell you that's why some of us were wanting to come over here.''

"Why?"

"Because if your old man wanted you back so badly we wanted to see why, and then there was rumour going around that you said the crack was ninety over here.''

"Maybe I did."

147

"Well it's not; look at us here sitting outside that dump there in a sausage van."

"Then there you are: I must be some way like the da, I don't always say it the straight way round."

"Now, Murphy, you're talking like Shuckersucker."

"Anyway, Jody, why are you and the lads so keen on doing this job?"

"Weren't we talking last night to you about it?"

"I don't remember too much about it."

"You told us about your girlfriend didn't you? First ever time you had one."

"Yea, I must have."

"And the other fellah, what's his name – Laughsky!"

"Oh, Flarsky!"

"So it just seemed the natural thing to do – Hey! It's getting dark now, we want to be on our toes."

And I can see what he means. The scrapyard beside us has closed and the workers have gone home. We stop talking for a while as we watch the dark coming in, and from where we are sitting Baulox is a weird place at night. There is a ferocious smell of molten plastic and boiled sausage. Like when you burn the handle of the teapot when you're opening a can of dog food. There is a constant humming and battering away in the distance like a chain battling down an endless coal hole, or a train trying to bash its way through a soft lead wall.

In front of us the Goosshitch Area is turning itself slowly into a horror film in the dark. Nothing moves in there except the imagination and terror. Away over to the East the city is flickering on like slow motion sparklers. Red warning lights flash on. Searchlights revolve. Square patches of yellow puff on and off in the grey. And over near the Baulox Highway a row of monster chimneys puff out a sort of fluorescent smoke.

And then there is a sort of puff and nearly as far as my eyes can see everywhere goes coal black. For a few seconds I feel a big astonishment. Maybe I didn't really think Micko could turn out the lights. I feel a bit afraid.

"This is it!" says Jody. "Grab the tools!"

"Can't see a thing!"

"Come on! Come on! Open the door, get those pliers!"

Forty-One

I'm a bit surprised at how bossy Jody gets, giving out orders like a hungover beet factory foreman: do this and do that. Jazus! It's nearly as bad as working in the Registry of Mortgages.

"Now cut the wire up along there, Paddy – no there!"

"I can hardly see a thing."

"Come on, Paddy, no messing! Do you want to have us all shot?"

"Alright," says I snipping away like a starving hen at the fence. Jody is cutting away at the other side and even with all his directions he's working faster than I am. Somehow he is able to see in the dark.

"That'll do!" he says.

"Augh! I'm after cutting my hand."

"Come on, get into the van!"

"Easy on!" says I, running for the passenger door, and then we're in and slamming the doors. There's a pause while he searches for the starter key.

"Come on, you little bastard!" he says, and we're going. He rams in the gears, and as far as I can see we drive straight into an inky blackness. There is a loud crunching and scraping, and the engine shudders and stops. He starts up again, revs up, goes back a bit, and drives forward. This time there is a clasping noise as the fence gives and the van lurches into the Goosshitch Area.

We drive along fairly slow and gradually I begin to make out shapes in the dark as the shadows loom up on us and batlike creatures flutter against the windows. I'm scared stiff but I don't like to tell Jody in case I'm imagining things. Then there is a peculiar shrieking sound as a large black object flies past us.

"Did you see that?" says I.

"What?" says Jody.

"The thing that went by us there."

"Nothing went by us! Everything in here is dead!"

And suddenly I'm bursting for a piss. I don't like the word DEAD.

"Can you stop – I want to get out for a piss," says I.

"Do it on the floor."

"I can't do it in here."

"Listen," says Jody, "we're grown up now and we can piss where we want to, so don't be afraid to piss your pants. Not to get shot is our job. Now, I reckon the Works is a half a mile over that way, along that road we pointed out."

"No, it's straight ahead!" says I not knowing why I'm so sure. And also I'm thinking of something else, about what Jody said. It was one of the things I had been afraid of all my life – pissing in my pants.

"You're right!" says Jody, "I can see the track now."

"Yea, straight on!" says I, and I take out my prick and piss on the floor.

"You'd think you could hold on for a toilet!" says Jody laughing.

"Sure," says I, but again I'm thinking of something else – I'm thinking that I, Paddy Murphy, have grown up at last, and I'm right slap bang in the middle of the Goosshitch Area on my way to steal the Essential Ingredient for a nuclear bomb. It's a queer sensation and my head is full of echoes – other people's advice, the voices of teachers, priests, brothers and little sayings. "Think before you act!" says a voice from the past.

"D'ye think we're doing the right thing, Jody?" says I.

"Course we're doing the right thing."

"We could go back to Dublin and forget about it," says I.

"And what about Micko and Lips! I'm not going back to them without finishing the job."

"It's not really our bomb!" says I.

"It's as much ours as anyone else's so stop cracking up your mind about it. It's best we have this Vital Ingredient in our pocket – we're hardly going to set it off on ourselves. That's why they make bombs, to blow people like us up. You don't think they'd use it on themselves."

"Yea," says I but I'm not enthusiastic. My mind is racing around other things. Maybe I should have listened more carefully to to the da.

"Is that the place?" says Jody, jerking me back into reality. And once again the fear is on me because we're almost there.

"Yea," says I.

"D'ye know, Murphy, you're not yourself today. You should have heard you last night – the fires of hell wouldn't have stopped you getting this Vital Ingredient," says Jody and drives straight over to the fence and cuts off the engine. It's sinister quiet outside except for a small wind.

"So that's the kip you work in!" says Jody.

"Yea."

"Strange looking joint! Come on, we'd better shift it. Grab the tools again."

This time we've only to make a fairly small hole but as we're cutting I spot a flashlight about two hundred yards inside the fence.

"There's a guard in there!" says I.

"Ah don't mind him, he won't hear a thing. Anyway he'd hardly be expecting anyone to break into this hole — anyone in their right mind!"

"You might be right."

"There, that should do. We should be able to get a bomb out through that. Now you lead the way to this Klam factory."

"It's over this way I think."

We head across a large open space towards the back of a long low building, and as we are creeping past this we almost bump into two gunmen who are standing at the doorway of a glass hut smoking and listening to the radio. Dast Fumptar Stoonk is playing.

"Good job they smoke cigars!" says Jody, and we skip back the way and around by another building, and suddenly I see the Klam Klam Perimeter. And my heart shoots — that's where I was shot.

"Where do they keep this ingredient?" says Jody.

"Just over there."

"By that wire gadget?"

"Yea, in the shed behind it."

"Well come on, we're nearly half way home then," he says, as a sliver of moon sneaks out from the clouds over BB-Sector.

"What are you staring at?"

"Just looking at the moon," says I. We move across to the building and I'm half expecting the alarm to go wild, but it stays quiet except for Dast Fumptar Stoonk.

"All the bloody doors are locked," says Jody as we feel our way around the building. He kicks at one or two but they are solid steel.

"And there are no windows to smash," he says.

"We'll never get in," says I.

"Paddy, we're not leaving here until we do! Hey, I told you, look at this!"

"What?" says I without interest. I'm shivering cold now and want to go home. When I move over to see what he's talking about I find him banging his knuckles against a big thick pipe that is sticking out from the wall.

"Well what d'ye know! It's made of plastic."

"So what?" says I.

"Plastic! It's like your heart, Murphy – it'll break. Now stand back."

He steps back himself then, makes a run at the pipe and gives it a ferocious thump with the heel of his boot. Crack! He kicks it again. I don't know what to do for he's obviously gone around the twist.

"Easy on, Jody," says I.

"Shush!" he says and this time he jumps at the pipe with both feet and there is a loud scrunching noise as the whole pipe comes from the wall, and a load of white goo comes spurting out.

"They'll hear us," says I.

"What a place to find milk!" says Jody. And the white stuff keeps flowing out of the pipe like a milk waterfall on a chocolate advertisement. Just when I'm thinking it will never stop it slows down to a dribble.

"Okay," says Jody, "one of us will have to get in through that."

"Are you serious?"

"Of course I'm serious."

"It's too narrow."

"Rubbish!"

I don't like the look of the hole in the wall. Once inside there might be no way out.

"Alright, we'll toss for it to see who goes in first."

"Alright."

"Well, give us one of those pumperknuckles or whatever you call them – I haven't as much as a bean. Pidgeon took all my money."

And there we go. Jody tosses the coin.

"Heads."

"Tails!" says Jody. "I win."

I don't want to climb into the little hole at all but I make what the da calls a tentative approach and stick my head gingerly through the opening. I can't see a thing inside but there's a funny smell of boiling glue coming off the white stuff. I feel Jody's hand on my bum as he's getting ready to give me a push.

"In you go!" says Jody.

"Hang on a second, I can't see a thing in here. I could easily drown in this stuff."

"Alright, I'll go in first. We haven't got all night."

"No, you won the toss," says I. I squeeze my shoulders into the pipe and by the time Jody heaves there is no going back. I slide forward along the pipe and suddenly the whole thing breaks, and I fall with a splash into

152

a big pool of the stuff. It's cold and sticky and comes up to my waist, and suddenly I know what claustrophobia is. I'm in some sort of a metal tank, in a panic and about to scream when I hear Jody laughing outside.

"Paddy," he says.

"What?" says I holding back the fright.

"Your old man. . . Do you know what he called me when I tried to get my bike back from him?"

"Ah Jody, listen. . ."

"He called me an obnoxious bollocks!"

"He did not, the da doesn't use bad language. And Jody, I can't get out of here."

"Well hold on, I'm coming in," he says, and next moment there's a fierce clatter as another bit of the pipe breaks and he lands in the pool beside me.

"Jesus wept, Paddy! You could have warned me that there was a bleeding lake down here."

"Are you alright?" says I.

"Course I'm alright," says Jody. "Strike a match!"

"It might blow up?" says I.

"How would it blow up! It's only milk of magnesia, the stuff that makes you shit more. Wouldn't you know by the taste of it?"

Clip! I strike one of the da's matches and what a sight! Jody's eyes are peering out crazy from a lumpy white mask. We're like two mice stuck at the bottom of a huge can of white paint.

"We'll never get out of here," says I, and for once Jody doesn't disagree with me. We're in a circular vat of some sort and the wall around us is about fifteen foot high. The match fizzles out.

"Strike another one!" says Jody.

"They're all wet now," says I.

"Well then, give me a hoosh up there and I'll get over the top."

I join my hands together, he puts his boot into them, grabs a hold of the back of my neck, climbs up on my shoulders, and he is trying to stand on my head when he lets out a curse, and falls on his ear back into the pool. But one thing about Jody, he doesn't give up that easy.

"It's harder than getting into Croke Park! Come on, give us a hoosh up again," he says breathing heavy. We do the same trick again only this time he succeeds in balancing on my head before making the jump, and then I hear him laughing.

"I've fucking made it!" he grunts and I hear him clambering crazy up the wall, and falling with a bang into a pile of metal cans or something

153

on the other side. For a while I hear him rooting about on the other side and then something fetches me a bang on the back of the head, and there is a splash.

"Oh God!" says I.

"It's only a ladder!" says Jody.

"You nearly skulled me!" says I grabbing the ladder and propping it up against the wall of the tank. I waste no time in climbing out of the stinking pool but as I arrive at the top I discover a terrifying scene. Somehow or other Jody has managed to open the main door to the warehouse, and the moon is shining in. It's ghostlike and cold, and a long black chain with a huge hook on the end of it is dangling from the roof. It looks like it's dripping out of the moon.

Resting on a rectangular splash of moonlight on the floor is a large wire basket, and inside this on a bed of straw is a shiny metallic object. It's sort of cylinder shaped with knobs and levers sticking out of it. It can only be the Essential Ingredient. And there beside it with his hand on it is Jody, with a crazy grin on his face. For a second I'm sure who he is – the devil! Jody is the devil!

"Get down out of that!" he says. "We haven't got all night."

Forty-Two

I nearly fall back off the ladder thinking he is the devil, but there's nothing I can do. I climb over to give him a hand. I'm shivering goosepimples and ready to obey his orders – what else can I do? We don't have to say anything about the bomb for we know what it is without talking. It's almost as if it was waiting for us. Jody grabs one end, and I the other, and we struggle out into the open. It's a bloody heavy yoke but everything seems to have been planned out somehow – a wheelbarrow is waiting outside for us. Without speaking we plop the baby into the barrow, and Jody signals for me to push while he leads the way. And off we go with me trying desperately to balance the bomb in the barrow – it keeps on wanting to keel over to the left, and I'm wondering should I drop it and run. Jody seems to read my mind.

"Keep a tight grip on that barrow, we're almost home," says Jody. And then the whole world goes terrifying bananas – lights flare up all over the gaff, the Klam Klam alarm screams off, and a huge searchlight starts revolving slowly around the Works. In a way it doesn't surprise me because I know I'm in hell.

"Quick!" says Jody, and we hurry to the fence as more and more lights come on – the whole place is beginning to look like an inferno, but nobody seems to be shining lights our way, and it's no trouble to get the barrow through the fence and into the van. All the confusion seems to be on the Baulox Highway side of the Works.

"Come on, let's get to hell out of here!" says Jody and we get in and drive away. Now that the electricity has been turned on the Goosshitch Area looks even weirder than it did, but I don't care for I feel resigned to the whole thing.

"We've done it, Murphy!" Jody keeps on saying, and I don't say anything. When we're about half way across the area Jody stops the van and turns off the engine. There is a deadly silence.

"What's up, Murphy?" asks Jody.

"There's no way out," says I in a whisper.

"Yes there is. Come on! Let's clean all this white stuff off us."

Jody finds some paper bags in the back of the van and cleans off his face, and all the time he keeps on talking about Dublin and what we're going to do when we get back. It's funny but I had almost forgotten about Dublin.

"How do I look?" says Jody turning to me but I can't see him properly in the dark.

"Will we ever go home?" says I.

"Course we will, now wipe off your face and head, we can't drive through town looking like this – black and white minstrels."

"Okay," says I, and there is a little bit of hope appearing in my mind. Maybe Jody isn't the devil. And maybe we're not in hell.

"You're very quiet, Paddy."

"Are you the devil?" says I.

"Are you losing your mind or something?" says Jody.

"No."

"You sound like my uncle who they locked up. What's your name?"

"Paddy Murphy."

"Well then, you're alright – you know who you are. Who am I?"'

"Jody."

"Jody who?"

"Jody McGovern."

"Okay, you're sane," he says, and he starts up the engine again.

"I was only joking," says I.

"About what?" says Jody.

"About you being the devil," says I.

"Well it wasn't funny," says Jody.

Forty-Three

It doesn't take us too long to get back to the hole in the fence, but as we're driving away from the Goosshitch Area we run into trouble. Up ahead of us are four cars blocking the road and a swarm of soldiers with a huge sign in the middle of the road – HORK! (Please stop!)

"Oh Jazus!" says Jody, and he turns the van around in a big U-turn, and we go back the other way. Then there is a sound of Zlip! Zlip! Clash! The small mirror at the side of the van breaks into little pieces.

"Mama!" says Jody. "The fucking eejits are shooting at us. . . And they're coming after us too."

"Are they catching us?" says I.

"Course they're catching us, this van of sausages isn't too hot. Hey! That's an idea – get in the back, Paddy, and start pegging things out at them."

"The bomb?"

"No, everything else – the wheelbarrow, the sausages. . . quick!" I climb over the seat into the back, and the next thing is I go sprawling and hit my head an awful wallop on the bomb. I can't see what's happening – we're skidding and swerving all over the place.

"Open the back door!" Jody shouts. It takes me a while to get back to the door and open it, and it starts banging like crazy but I catch a glimpse of what's coming after us: two army lorries spanning the width of the road with blue revolving lights on top and sirens screeching. I throw out a tray of Giant Hot Dogs, the spare wheel, a toolbox, a tray of sausages, the wheelbarrow, and more stuff. . .

"Look out!" Jody shouts. The van takes a wild swerve and I end up on my ear again, gawking out through the back door of the van at a most amazing crash. It's unreal, like a slow motion stock car pile-up. A big red bus appears out of nowhere going the opposite direction to us and heading straight for the army lorries. It slews across the road, folds itself up like a melodeon, and next minute there are bits of wheelbarrow, sausages, lorries, guns, screams, all sorts of of stuff up in the air and flying all over the place.

"That was a close shave," says Jody. I shut the door best as I can and

157

climb back into the front seat. I'm all wobbly at the knees and dizzy in the stomach. I might get sick or faint or pass out or puke or do anything. I don't feel well.

"That should keep them busy sorting out that mess. Maybe they'll leave us alone now," says Jody, but I don't listen too much or talk back. After a while I notice that Jody has somehow managed to drive into the slums. I can tell that by the dogs on the pavement. Nowhere else in Baulox East or West will you see a dog. They are strictly FOKTERSHNEITENHAPST! (Illegal).

"How did you get in here?" says I.

"Just took the skinniest and darkest roads," says Jody.

"Well, we can drop the bomb off here – Kamam lives here."

"I don't care where Cowman lives, we're taking the Vital Ingredient back to show the lads!"

"But he's the leader of the LLL."

"Well Micko and the lads will have to have a look at it first. How do we get to the local from here?"

"I'm not sure, but I'd say it's that way! To the left there."

Forty-Four

METAL EGG.

Jody doesn't find it as easy to get out of the slums as he did to get in. He keeps on driving down cul-de-sacs.

"An interesting place," he says, "a bit like parts of Dublin."

"Yea, they allow dogs around here, and they let kids play on the streets."

"Can kids not play any other place?"

"I've never seen them," says I.

Again he has to do a U-turn at the bottom of a cul-de-sac, takes a right, takes a left, takes another left, and then I see the four big chimneys belonging to DAF GUMSWEINERTOSAK INTERNATIONAL-WEK F.L. (The International French Letter Consortium).

"I know where I am – it's over that way, keep left," says I.

"Right you be," says Jody. We bear left past the SOMMT KUMMT FATT G.T.W. (Drug factory) and on past the KOCX (Don't know what they do). It's easy enough going after that and we join the main stream of traffic flowing into the East Sector, but on the Baulox Highway we come to another army blockade. Jody is halfway across the road in a panicky U-turn until I tell him they're only stopping traffic going the other way.

"Good," says he straightening out the van. Sure enough, the two soldiers on our side of the road don't even look at us because they're straining their eyes to see what's happening behind them where the army have stopped a couple of hundred cars. One of them waves us on, and Jody waves back at him with a big grin.

It only takes a few minutes to get to The Harbour Bar and we get a laughing reception when we come in. Pidgeon and Stabber are sitting in the corner with the drunks and they nearly fall out of their chairs when they see us. The drunks seem to find us funny as well although they don't seem to be as mesmeric as usual. One or two of them are watching us like hawks.

"Is it snowing out?" is the first question we're asked, and when I look closer at Jody I see what Stabber means. The white milk of magnesia has dried itself out like cotton wool and the pair of us must look daft.

"Where is Micko?" says Jody, and he spots him before anyone

answers. Lips and himself are in the quiet part of the bar playing draughts. Jody gives him a wink and a left hand thumb up signal, and we go upstairs to clean ourselves up. I don't think Mister Echolle has even seen us coming into the bar, but I'm not sure.

After a hard scrub and a change of clothes we go down to join the lads in the bar who are curious as hell about the bomb.

"Bring it into the bar!" Pidgeon keeps saying.

"Shush!" says Jody, but there's no containing them, so Jody and myself and Lips go out and slip the Essential Ingredient in through the kitchen door and up to my room. It was some job getting it up the stairs but we managed it alright without anyone seeing us. And we are no sooner in the room than the rest of the lads are crowding in wanting to look at it.

"So that's the Essential!" says Lips.

"It looks like a metal egg that's suffered an abortion," says Pidgeon, who can come out with a few flowery words when he's had a few.

"A Martian's tit!" says Stabber.

"Let's put it on the bed," says Jody.

"Ah no, I want to sleep there," says I.

"No sleep until we get rid of it," says Jody, and himself and Lips plonk it down on the bed. It does look a bit like a metal egg gone wrong.

"We'll have to sober some of youz up," says Jody and goes down to the kitchen to make some tea and sandwiches. He comes back up immediately with a big pile of documents and photographs.

"Look what I found in the freezer!" he says.

"You found nothing," says I. "They're mine. I knocked them off the army when I came here first and hid them behind Missus Echolle's six month supply of butter."

"And what are they all about?" says Jody. That's one thing about him — he's a ferocious curiosity about other people's business.

"See this one — what does that say?" he asks, and he doesn't let up until I've translated most of them for him. He seems very interested in the Eight Sane Men.

Forty-Five

DAF NUCLEROMO BADUUMECHINZIST.

"So why don't we give the Vital Ingredient to the Sane People?" says Jody.

"I promised it to the LLL," says I.

"Didn't you tell us yourself that some of them are a bit touched?"

"The fellah in control is a bit out of it alright."

"This Cowman guy?"

"Kamam, yea."

"Why don't we toss for it then? Heads, we give it to the Sane People, tails or harps we give it to Cowman?"

"Alright."

"But it doesn't seem right to me," says Hairlips.

"Why not Lips?" asks Jody.

"Not after all the trouble we had in getting it," says Lips.

"Well, who do you think should have the Vital Ingredient?"

"I'd go for the Live and Liberation gang!" says Micko.

"We could vote on it," says Lips.

"Good idea," says Stabber.

"Okay, we'll toss to see who votes first," says Jody.

And we toss and Micko wins first vote. He likes the sound of the LLL; he votes for them. So do I. Lips goes for the Eight Sane Men. Pidgeon goes for the Eight as well. Stabber goes LLL; and Jody has the last vote. "I vote," says Jody, "that we all go out now and meet the Sane People."

"And leave the bomb in the bed?" says I, thinking about Missus Echolle finding it.

"It'll be safe enough," says Jody.

"D'ye think we should all go?" says Stabber.

"I think someone should cover the bar, just in case," says Pidgeon.

"Okay," says Jody. "Who has the tickets?"

"What time are we heading out anyway?"

"First thing in the morning, seven hundred and. . ."

"Quarter past seven."

"Okay, Pidgeon stays behind to cover the bar. . . and Stabber, you may as well too."

The rest of us get into Jody's van and drive down by the Swurge River where Micko finds out from an upper-class whore that Greenbogger Gardens is back a bit towards the airport. It's a fairly swanky area and Greenbogger turns out to be one of those public cul-de-sacs that people don't like you walking into. Number 40 is way up the back of it, and it's built different to all the other houses on the road. It's a bit like an upside down teapot with a glass roof, and one side going off at a slant. There is a blue candle burning in one of the side windows.

"A strange looking kip for Sane People to be living in," says Jody.

"Don't look, but there's two men in a car on the other side of the road," says Micko.

"Probably Branch," says Jody, "but we've nothing to hide; come on, let's meet these Sane People." And he turns the van straight up into their driveway and crunches to a stop on the pebbles beside what looks to me to be a car from the old days. We troop out across the lawn and around the side where we find the doorway. Jody presses the red electric bell-button which goes ding-dong, and a dog barks inside.

"Thought dogs were against the law," says Micko.

"They are, but these are Sane People," says Jody.

"Hallo," says I as a doddery old man with grey hair opens the door. He's carrying a walking stick and looks like he could do with a solid meal.

"Vurster kun grapester slamt eigen?" (Can I assist you?) he says.

"Can you talk ordinary?" says Jody. The old man stares suspiciously at us, first at me, then at Micko, then at our car, then off down the road, and decides something to himself.

"Please come in," he says and we follow him into a very wooden kitchen where there are seven men sitting around a long rectangular table playing cards. The funny thing is they seem to be playing in two groups.

"You must be the Eight Sane Men," say Jody, taking out the documents and photographs and putting them on the table. It doesn't take them too long to figure out what they are.

"Where did you get these? And what exactly are you looking for?" says one of the younger Sane Men.

"We're looking for nothing," says Jody. "We want to know if you want the Vital Ingredient."

"Vital ingredient for what, may I ask?" says this guy again. He speaks like the guy I talked to on the phone but he seems a lot tougher for some reason. Jody doesn't seem to be getting on too well with him.

"We're asking if you want it, that's all!" says Jody.

"But what is IT, my young man."

"Paddy, you tell him," says Jody.

"It's Daf Einfanb from the Works," says I, and you'd almost swear a bomb went off in the room.

"Daf Nucleromo Baduumechinzist!" says the guy at the far end of the table. It's a new one to me.

"Okay, if you don't want it, we'll go," says Jody and we make towards the door. And that starts them all talking at once in a big confusion of Baulox. The younger man calls us back.

It seems they want Daf Einfanb very badly. They think it might be the very thing they need for some negotiations they are having with the government. They want us to hold a Moostar Geragma immediately.

This Mooster Geragma turns out to be fairly painful. First we have to suffer a pile of introductions and handshakes and some woeful bad tea that tastes like stinging nettles. Then we've to sit around the long table and listen to a load of horrible political spoof. Words like UNILATERAL and DEPRIVED MINORITY are thrown all over the room. It's like a big fog escaped out of a dictionary and there would be no way out except that in the end Hairlips gets pissed off with all the wogglewash and comes up with a plan.

It's a simple enough plan and it brings a lot of relief to the Eight Sane Men. Me and Jody and the lads would go back out to the van and bring the Baulox Special Branch on a wild goose chase. The Eight Sane Men would get a lorry or van or something and drive to The Harbour Bar. There we'd hand over the Essential Ingredient. And Bob's your missus! We'd be back in Dublin before we knew it.

We all agree it's a grand plan, and sure enough as we drive away from Greenbogger Gardens the Special Branch come after us.

"They're after us!" says Jody with a big grin and his boot pressing the accelerator down to the floor. Then he slows up. Waits for the Branch to catch up on us. Drives carefully then. Does a right. Takes a left. Makes sure all his traffic signals are correct. And then suddenly stops at an intersection where there are five roads.

"This is it! Take a road each," says Jody as the other car pulls in behind us. There are two men in it.

"Okay," says Jody. "Take a deep breath and count to ten." We're standing on the pavement outside the car and I doubt if the two men following us know what we're at. Naturally we pretend we don't know they're there.

". . .five, six, seven, eight, nine, ten!" says Jody. We wave at an imaginary person in the van, and start walking slowly away in four different directions. And then we're all running as fast as we can go – the rule is you have to walk ten yards before you break into a sprint. The Baulox Special Branch wouldn't have a chance of catching us because we're all good runners. We had to do that trick in Dublin once or twice.

Nobody even comes after me and after a while I slow down to a walk and head casually in the direction of The Harbour Bar.

Forty-Six

The Harbour Bar seems to be more crowded with drunks than I ever remembered. Some of them actually wave at me when I come in. Their corner is hardly able to hold them all in it, and I see Pidgeon is among them entertaining them to a jig with his comb. None of the other lads are there. Pidgeon doesn't even notice me when I walk through and go up to my room.

"You made it, Murphy!" says Jody, and I'm relieved to see all the lads are there.

"It's a wonder you're not down with Pidgeon in the bar," says I.

"We're shagged out!" says Lips.

"Yea, and so am I," says I and sit down against the wall between Stabber and Micko. Nobody seems to want to say anything. We're all sitting around like so many cooped-up chickens with the Essential Ingredient sitting up in the bed in front of us like an ugly duck egg waiting to be hatched. I can sense everyone is starting to get nervous like the last two minutes in the dressing room before the hurling final gets going. We've only a few hours left before our flight, and any second the Eight Sane Men should arrive to pick up the bomb. Even Jody is biting his fingernails, but it's he who breaks the silence in the end.

"The thing I can't understand," he says, "is what are these Sane People going to do with it?"

"I don't know," says I.

"They didn't seem all that sane to me! They don't even know how to make a cup of tea," says Jody.

"I think the Live and Liberate bunch would be better," says Micko.

"It's a bit late now," says I.

"I wonder," says Jody. "What do you think, Hairlips?"

"Yea, I've been thinking about it," says Lips.

"And what have you come up with?" says Micko.

"It seems to me," says Lips, "that the safest thing to do would be to bring it home with us and put it in some place very secure − like your old man's shed or somewhere.

Jazus! It's as if Hairlips had said something magic − everybody wakes up all at once.

165

"That's a brilliant idea!" says Stabber. And everyone else nods their heads in agreement. I seem to be the only one with any doubts about it.

"That's settled then!" says Jody.

"But we'd never get that colossus through the customs — it sticks out about two hundred miles," says I.

"Yea," says Jody and the excitement dies down again. We'd have to give it to the Eight Sane Men.

"There must be some way," says Stabber without thinking one up. And nobody else seems to have an idea either.

"What do you think, Hairlips?" says Jody.

"The way I see it," says Lips, "it might be a good idea to have it sticking out like a sore prick."

"I don't get you," says I.

"Then we wouldn't have to hide it — just take it onto the plane as it is," says Lips.

"Ah, come off it!" says Micko. "They'd think it was a bomb."

"It is a bomb," says I.

"It wouldn't have to be," says Lips. "We could dress it up!" And at that we all break out laughing except for Hairlips who doesn't see the humour in his idea.

"Sure!" says Jody. "Put a skirt on it — my deformed sister! Don't say anything about her deformity, it's not her fault. She was born that way. We're taking her to Matt Talbot's Shrine and then on to Lourdes."

"No, serious!" says Lips.

"Yea!" says Jody. "And how do you explain she hasn't a passport and has a face like a nuclear bomb?"

"That's the thing," says Lips. "It could be one of those things the artists put in museums and outside banks."

"Sure! Looks like a painting doesn't it?" says Jody.

"I've seen weirder things than that outside banks," says Lips.

"Sculpture!" says Micko.

"Jazus, you're right!" says Jody getting the idea. And suddenly Jody goes all bossy like he did earlier outside the Goosshitch Area. He starts shouting out orders.

"I'll be the sculpture man," says Jody.

"The sculpturer," says Micko.

"The sculptur. . .ure," says Jody finding the word impossible to pronounce but it doesn't stop him from knowing what he's doing. He gives out the orders like he was fucking Julius Caesar back to haunt us:

Stabber and Pidgeon are to go outside and raid the bins, collect any old sort of junk, metal, cardboard, dead dogs, paint, plastic, anything. Me and Micko are to stay behind and look after the Eight Sane Men, get them pissed, or get rid of them, tell them the bomb is going to blast off, tell them anything, and keep a look out for the cops. He and Hairlips are to go out and liberate a suitable car to bring a famous sculpture-man and his followers to the airport. And then, to beat the band, Stabber is to get hold of some inks and make him out a little placard, or a big one, whatever he thinks:

JODY McGOVERN PUMPOSTEITER GOOTZ FACT-ERTRASHNING EISTER INTERNATIONALWEK BAULOX GUMPT (Jody McGovern winner of first prize at Baulox International Sculpture Exhibition).

And then the four of them are gone out in a frantic hurry to execute orders. Me and Micko are left holding the fort but it's not long before we have to do something – Missus Echolle comes bursting into the room; she is full of questions.

"Who are all those men in the lorry outside?" she says. "What! What is that on the bed?"

"Don't worry," says Micko. "That's only an Irish vacuum cleaner."

"And the men outside," says I, "are workmates of mine. They've come for the big celebration. Micko, you go down and invite them in for a drink."

"That is good," says Missus Echolle when he goes out, "that you bring good custom to the bar. Not since the Resistance had we business like this. But what is that?"

"Ah, it's just a gadget for work. I'll have it out of here tomorrow."

"Good, you take that away! I do not like it. It is bad enough with my husband's hobbies without. . . Now I had better go down and help him with the bar."

"Right you be," says I and wait until Jody comes back before I go down myself. Jazus! The place is nearly packed out to the door. It's a small world – somehow the da has arrived in and he's getting on like two convent girls with Darold Schnapter, the oldest Sane Man and homosexual vegetarian. The other Sane Men are cluttered in a tight pack around Micko at the bar. And to beat it all, who comes in only one of the LLL, Skinnyface with the blond hair and big shoes; and in after him, I don't believe it, comes Blumm's secretary, Manda Zeriniski. Within seconds the da and the vegetarian have cornered Manda and are beginning to pour drinks into her. As usual she's wearing very little clothes and a big smile.

Mister and Missus Echolle are in a tizzy trying to keep up with the demand for drink. It's strange, but the drunks in the corner seem to resent this invasion of their privacy – they have gathered around in a sort of a band with their backs to everyone else. And maybe I'm mistaken, because two of them wave over at me. And then Micko is calling for me. I try and go over but Manda jumps up from her chair and grabs my elbow. It's like a madhouse!

"Paddy, I must talk to you."

"Sure."

"You've taken it, I don't know how."

"Taken what?"

"Daf Einfanb!" she whispers.

"Yea, I'll get it over to you tomorrow."

"We may need it sooner."

"Who would want that bloody thing?"

"You know we have claimed responsibility?"

"Why would you do that?" says I.

"I don't think you understand politics, Herr Murphy."

"I don't want to," says I and turn away from her. I feel like spluttering into tears but Micko comes over.

"Look after that nut!" he says, inching his head towards Irvork's back.

"What's up?" says I, inching my head at Manda.

"D'ye know what he's drinking – bleeding banana juice!" says Micko.

"Paddy!" shouts the da.

"Scuse me," says I going over to him with Manda after me.

"Take a seat there, Miss Zeriniski," says the da, and bloody hell then if he doesn't ignore me altogether. I go on over to Micko who's back talking to Irvork, the youngest Sane Man, who I find is in a frantic hurry.

"We cannot wait much longer. You must hand it over!"

"Okay, just wait there; come on, Micko, we'll try and organise it," says I and we make for the stairs.

"Paddy," Manda calls.

"I'll be right back," says I.

Jody's going wild in the room upstairs with red paint, and somehow or other he has stuck a pair of handlebars onto the bomb, and feathers and ugh!. . . Stabber is busy printing out a very official looking sign, and Pidgeon and Lips are looking on.

"Pidgeon," says I, "can you go down and entertain them some more down there."

"Can you not stand the pace?" says Pidgeon.

"No, somebody has to keep an eye downstairs. Don't want the da coming up here or something."

"Right you be, I could do with a drink," says Pidgeon.

"Only an hour and a half left to take-off," says Lips.

"Must be more than that," says I.

"No."

"Shut up!" says Jody. "You're disturbing the work!"

"Christ! Do you have to make it look so sick? Jazus, it was bad enough as it was."

"That was only the outside," says Jody. "What I'm doing is painting the inside back out on the outside."

"What are you going to call it?" says Lips.

"Duck's Head," says Jody giving us a bit of a laugh; and then Stabber wants some admiration for his stuff as well.

"What d'ye think of it?" says he.

"Game ball!" says Lips. And I have to admit Stabber's placard has the strokes of genius. It looks as important as a supermarket coupon with a little bit of something extra in it.

"Now for to let it dry out," says Jody rubbing his hands together. I can see he's proud of himself.

"I think I'll go down for a drink," says Stabber. "One for the road."

"Hold on," says I.

"What's up?" says Stabber.

"There's LLL and Sane Men all over the kip! We'll have to get rid of them."

"Right! We'll tell them the bomb is about to burst!" says Jody.

"I don't know," says Lips.

"Why not?" says Jody.

"Someone might send in the bomb squad."

"And what should we do?" says Micko.

"Sneak it out?" says Jody.

"That might be hard," says Lips.

"Then what?"

"We could call up the cops, or maybe the army on the phone?"

"What!" says Jody. "Fucking traitor!"

"No, I didn't mean it that way. What I was thinking was what would happen if they knew downstairs that we called the cops?"

"You call the cops and I'll lambaste ye!" says Jody.

"Some of them might leave," says Lips.

"I'm fucking sure some of them might leave!" says Jody. "And you'd leave too with a broken head."

"He means only a pretend phone call," says Micko.

"Get it!" says Jody with a wild gleam coming in his eyes. And again he starts giving orders. First Micko has to go down and fetch up Pidgeon. And while he's down there he may as well look worried. And then the whole six of us are to go down and spread the rumour like wildfire, that the cops are coming, that the army is on its way, that phone calls have been made, search warrants, all sorts of junk, and then see what sort of people stay drinking in the bar.

"They're getting itchy pants down there!" says Pidgeon when he comes in.

"Shush!" says Jody and tells him the story. And then we all slip down to see if we can spread a rumour. Pidgeon tells Herr Irvork of the Sane Men. I tell the da that it seems like the cops are coming over. Micko shouts out something about the army to the drunks. Stabber tells everyone that everyone is going to be arrested. Hairlips just acts very suspicious and makes a dart for the back stairs. That's all we do.

And the result is a miracle! Manda jumps up out of her chair and grabs my shoulder.

"Where is it?" she says.

"Pedra's bar," says I, thinking of the first place that came to mind, and then she's running out the door after Skinnyface with the blond hair and big shoes. The Eight Sane Men are cooler about it — they just leave down their drinks and disappear into the night.

"I thought Herr Blumm's secretary would have more manners than that!" says the da.

One or two of the drunks stagger out, but funny enough the rest of them all seem to sober up at once. I notice several of them reaching for bottles and glasses, and none of them seem to be drinking out of them. And the Echolles – they pull down the shutters at front and dim down the lights.

"Without a bye or leave," says the da," I don't know what got into the girl – surely we're not drinking after hours, Paddy?"

"No, it's a twenty-four hour licence," says I.

"Well, in that case you can buy me a drink – I'll try a little brandy and, what is the name of that vintage – Morschnort, that's it."

"They don't sell it here, da!"

"Well shagg then."

"Right you be, da," says I and get a couple of drinks. When I bring them back he wants me to sit down –

"I must have a serious conversation with you, Paddy."

"Yea?"

"About this sailing vacation. . ."

"But, da, we're all leaving in about ten minutes."

"And going where may I ask?"

"We're going back to Dublin – plane leaves at quarter past seven."

"Excellent! So you have decided to take an early holiday. In that instance I shall accompany you."

"Have you a ticket?"

"Damn tickets! I presume I can get one at the airport. Now, Paddy, calm yourself down, you appear to be all agitated."

"Yea, okay. How'ye, Jody!"

"Hia, Paddy: How's it cutting, Mister Murphy? Did you hear the news about me?" says Jody.

"I've an earful of bad news already thank you."

"I got first place in the show!" says Jody.

"That doesn't sound like bad news. What show?"

"The artist's competition: hey Micko, Hairlips, bring down the Duck's Head! Mister Murphy wants to see it before we go. And Pidgeon, bring around the car – I don't think I should drive seeing as I won."

"I can't drive!" says Pidgeon.

"I'll have to drive then," says Jody.

When the Essential Ingredient alias Duck's Head makes an appearance in the bar the drunks go bananas wanting to have a look at it. I never before seen them leaving their chairs for anything except drink. And I don't believe it – they stand in a ring around the thing clapping.

Even the da seems impressed and he pays particular attention to the placard hanging on the duck's neck.

"May I be the first to congratulate you!" says the da.

"Thanks," says Jody.

"Very therianthropic! I especially like your allusion to the wheel and even more explicitly to the bipedal. Are you part of the Post-Structuralist School?"

"No, I've gone past that," says Jody.

"Good, I never had too much time for it."

"Hey! We'd better shift it!" says Lips. The da looks at his watch.

"Yes, I'm afraid he's right. And now, my good friend, seeing as you are famous, I shall have the honour of driving. Keys?"

"Mister Murphy, that's great. The only bother is the key I have here is a bit of a makey-uppey one and you have to twiddle it a bit to get it going."

"Don't be worrying your head off — give it to me. I remember when I was half your age I used to have to start my father's tractor with a four inch nail."

"You never told me granda had a tractor!" says I.

"I had better things to tell you, Paddy!" says the da.

"Stop yabbering!" says Lips.

"Indeed we best go!" says the da.

Forty-Seven

THE FLY.

I don't think any of us ever arrived into an airport in such style, in the big yellow car that Jody thought would be suitable for the occasion. Mister and Missus Echolle and the drunks must have been surprised when the da pulled around to the front of The Harbour Bar in the big limousine shaped halfway between a rocket and a banana. It seemed to send the drunks delirious with laughing, but they gave us a good farewell and we all hoped they'd come over to Dublin one of these days.

When we get out in the airport the da is acting all erect and proud like he was the Jazus High King of Ireland. I never saw anything like – and as for Jody, he's grinning all over him and waving to imaginary people like he was the Pope on his way to Cuba or somewhere. Micko and Hairlips have to do the donkey work and carry the Essential Ingredient, but even they don't have to do that much because the da waves over a porter and soon Daf Einfanb or Duck's Head or whatever you call it is riding majestically towards the Departure Gate. Of course, with all this nonsense the da and Jody are getting into we soon have a crowd of men with cameras after us. They almost won't let us get on the plane and they keep shoving us into the area for celebrities where the puffier armchairs are. It seems that the only two celebrities in the house are Jody and Jixter Varnokker, lead singer of Koosh, who play Dast Fumptar Stoonk in the Baulox Hit Parade. And even at that the rumour is going around that this Jixter fellah is a has-been, but Jody is coming into his own.

However famous he is, we still have to flash tickets then, and there's a bit of a problem when the sculpture is weighed and again the da has to put in a spoof about Irish Art while explaining some stuff about combined weights. It sounds daft to me but it seems to work, and the girl gives us back Jody's sculpture with a big smile. There's nothing left to do then except go on down the passageway and into the plane. We don't even have to walk across the tarmac. It's just like going from one room to another.

People are inclined to think that planes glide smoothly into the air, but they don't – they usually stumble their way up into the sky, and this one is no exception. It lumbers awkwardly along the narrow black road, its wings trembling like they were going to fall off, and then it farts,

173

roars and jerks its huge clumsy body into the sky. I'd normally feel a touch of panic at this stage as everything is wrenched from my control, but I don't – I'm physically too tired, sick and suffering from a throbbing pain in my side to feel anything except wretched.

The other lads are in great form, but I don't really feel like taking part in their celebration or whatever you could call it. Once the microphone speaker tells us we can unbuckle our belts the lads start acting like they've won a football match. The da who is about six seats up from me immediately starts chatting up one of the hostess women, and the lads order drinks. I can't help but notice that the fame is going a bit to Jody's head – for some reason he doesn't seem to be the same friend I've known over a few years. He's shouting out of himself a bit louder than usual. He even says something about careers.

"Artists!" he says. "That's what we can be!"

"Piss artists!" says Micko.

"Serious!" says Jody, and I can see he has Hairlips chewing over the idea.

"Sure, look how simple it was to make that thing!" he says pointing to the bomb. And when I glance over I can see it is the most horrible object I've ever set my eyes on or dreamed about. He's painted a sort of duck skull on the top of it and out the eyes comes a load of blood and guts – it's crying blood. In a way I can see he's already grown into some sort of terrible artist, but the lads aren't as serious about it as he is.

"I suppose Hairlips will be a ballet dancer!" says Micko.

"I don't know," says Lips. "There might be something in it."

"And Murphy could be a writer!" says Jody. "Did you ever read the insults wrote on his essay?"

"Yea," says I, not believing a word or caring less. And then Jody gets a bit of his old self back and stops talking guff – he gets up to see if the pilot will let him drive the plane, and up at the front door he borrows a microphone and turns around to the passengers.

"This is your Captain talking," says Jody. "We are now leaving Baulox!"

And the big grin comes on his face and several people laugh, mostly the lads, but I don't feel much like it myself. I can't help looking over at the bomb that's resting across from me with its safety belt on. And it's unusual – a little black fly has got itself onto the plane and it's flying around the nose of the bomb. For some reason it makes me feel very small — the little fly in the big awkward aeroplane, and it not knowing where it's going, and us up in the air and flying over the earth, and the earth turning around some way, and twisting itself around the sun, and I can't help but wonder where we're all bound. . .